# THE STORY OF THE GLITTERING PLAIN

# WHICH HAS BEEN ALSO CALLED THE LAND OF LIVING MEN OR THE ACRE OF THE UNDYING

WRITTEN BY
WILLIAM MORRIS

# CHAPTER I: OF THOSE THREE WHO CAME TO THE HOUSE OF THE RAVEN

It has been told that there was once a young man of free kindred and whose name was Hallblithe: he was fair, strong, and not untried in battle; he was of the House of the Raven of old time.

This man loved an exceeding fair damsel called the Hostage, who was of the House of the Rose, wherein it was right and due that the men of the Raven should wed.

She loved him no less, and no man of the kindred gainsaid their love, and they were to be wedded on Midsummer Night.

But one day of early spring, when the days were yet short and the nights long, Hallblithe sat before the porch of the house smoothing an ash stave for his spear, and he heard the sound of horse-hoofs drawing nigh, and he looked up and saw folk riding toward the house, and so presently they rode through the garth gate; and there was no man but he about the house, so he rose up and went to meet them, and he saw that they were but three in company: they had weapons with them, and their horses were of the best; but they were no fellowship for a man to be afraid of; for two of them were old and feeble, and the third was dark and sad, and drooping of aspect: it seemed as if they had ridden far and fast, for their spurs were bloody and their horses all a-sweat.

Hallblithe hailed them kindly and said: "Ye are way-worn, and maybe ye have to ride further; so light down and come into the house, and take bite and sup, and hay and corn also for your horses; and then if ye needs must ride on your way, depart when ye are rested; or else if ye may, then abide here night-long, and go your ways to-morrow, and meantime that which is ours shall be yours, and all shall be free to you."

Then spake the oldest of the elders in a high piping voice and said: "Young man, we thank thee; but though the days of the springtide are waxing, the hours of our lives are waning; nor may we abide unless thou canst truly tell us that this is the Land of the Glittering Plain: and if that be so, then delay not, lead us to thy lord, and perhaps he will make us content."

Spake he who was somewhat less stricken in years than the first: "Thanks have thou! but we need something more than meat and drink, to wit the Land of Living Men. And Oh! but the time presses."

—

Spake the sad and sorry carle: "We seek the Land where the days are many: so many that he who hath forgotten how to laugh, may learn the craft again, and forget the days of Sorrow."

Then they all three cried aloud and said:

"Is this the Land? Is this the Land?"

But Hallblithe wondered, and he laughed and said: "Wayfarers, look under the sun down the plain which lieth betwixt the mountains and the sea, and ye shall behold the meadows all gleaming with the spring lilies; yet do we not call this the Glittering Plain, but Cleveland by the Sea. Here men die when their hour comes, nor know I if the days of their life be long enough for the forgetting of sorrow; for I am young and not yet a yokefellow of sorrow; but this I know, that they are long enough for the doing of deeds that shall not die. And as for Lord, I know not this word, for here dwell we, the sons of the Raven, in good fellowship, with our wives that we have wedded, and our mothers who have borne us, and our sisters who serve us. Again I bid you light down off your horses, and eat and drink, and be merry; and depart when ye will, to seek what land ye will."

They scarce looked on him, but cried out together mournfully:

"This is not the Land! This is not the Land!"

No more than that they said, but turned about their horses and rode out through the garth gate, and went clattering up the road that led to the pass of the mountains. But Hallblithe hearkened wondering, till the sound of their horse-hoofs died away, and then turned back to his work: and it was then two hours after high-noon.

# CHAPTER II: EVIL TIDINGS COME TO HAND AT CLEVELAND

Not long had he worked ere he heard the sound of horsehoofs once more, and he looked not up, but said to himself, "It is but the lads bringing back the teams from the acres, and riding fast and driving hard for joy of heart and in wantonness of youth."

But the sound grew nearer and he looked up and saw over the turf wall of the garth the flutter of white raiment; and he said:

"Nay, it is the maidens coming back from the sea-shore and the gathering of wrack."

So he set himself the harder to his work, and laughed, all alone as he was, and said: "She is with them: now I will not look up again till they have ridden into the garth, and she has come from among them, and leapt off her horse, and cast her arms about my neck as her wont is; and it will rejoice her then to mock me with hard words and kind voice and longing heart; and I shall long for her and kiss her, and sweet shall the coming days seem to us: and the daughters of our folk shall look on and be kind and blithe with us."

Therewith rode the maidens into the garth, but he heard no sound of laughter or merriment amongst them, which was contrary to their wont; and his heart fell, and it was as if instead of the maidens' laughter the voices of those wayfarers came back upon the wind crying out, "Is this the Land? Is this the Land?"

Then he looked up hastily, and saw the maidens drawing near, ten of the House of the Raven, and three of the House of the Rose; and he beheld them that their faces were pale and woe-begone, and their raiment rent, and there was no joy in them. Hallblithe stood aghast while one who had gotten off her horse (and she was the daughter of his own mother) ran past him into the hall, looking not at him, as if she durst not: and another rode off swiftly to the horse-stalls. But the others, leaving their horses, drew round about him, and for a while none durst utter a word; and he stood gazing at them, with the spoke-shave in his hand, he also silent; for he saw that the Hostage was not with them, and he knew that now he was the yokefellow of sorrow.

At last he spoke gently and in a kind voice, and said: "Tell me, sisters, what evil hath befallen us, even if it be the death of a dear friend, and the thing that may not be amended."

Then spoke a fair woman of the Rose, whose name was Brightling, and said: "Hallblithe, it is not of death that we have to tell, but of sundering, which may yet be amended. We were on the sand of the sea nigh the Ship-stead and the Rollers of the Raven, and we were gathering the wrack and playing together; and we saw a round-ship nigh to shore lying with her sheet slack, and her sail beating the mast; but we deemed it to be none other than some bark of the Fish-biters, and thought no harm thereof, but went on running and playing amidst the little waves that fell on the sand, and the ripples that curled around our feet. At last there came a small boat from the side of the round-ship, and rowed in toward shore, and still we feared not, though we drew a little aback from the surf and let fall our gown-hems. But the crew of that boat beached her close to where we stood, and came hastily wading the surf towards us; and we saw that they were twelve weaponed men, great, and grim, and all clad in black raiment. Then indeed were we afraid, and we turned about and fled up the beach; but now it was too late, for the tide was at more than half ebb and long was

—

5

the way over the sand to the place where we had left our horses tied among the tamarisk-bushes. Nevertheless we ran, and had gotten up to the pebble-beach before they ran in amongst us: and they caught us, and cast us down on to the hard stones.

"Then they made us sit in a row on a ridge of the pebbles; and we were sore afraid, yet more for defilement at their hands than for death; for they were evil-looking men exceeding foul of favour. Then said one of them: 'Which of all you maidens is the Hostage of the House of the Rose?'

"Then all we kept silence, for we would not betray her. But the evil man spake again: 'Choose ye then whether we shall take one, or all of you across the waters in our black ship.' Yet still we others spake not, till arose thy beloved, O Hallblithe, and said:

"'Let it be one then, and not all; for I am the Hostage.'

"'How shalt thou make us sure thereof?' said the evil carle.

"She looked on him proudly and said: 'Because I say it.'

"'Wilt thou swear it?' said he.

"'Yea,' said she, 'I swear it by the token of the House wherein I shall wed; by the wings of the Fowl that seeketh the Field of Slaying.'

"'It is enough,' said the man, 'come thou with us. And ye maidens sit ye there, and move not till we have made way on our ship, unless ye would feel the point of the arrow. For ye are within bowshot of the ship, and we have shot weapons aboard.'

"So the Hostage departed with them, and she unweeping, but we wept sorely. And we saw the small boat come up to the side of the round-ship, and the Hostage going over the gunwale along with those evil men, and we heard the hale and how of the mariners as they drew up the anchor and sheeted home; and then the sweeps came out and the ship began to move over the sea. And one of those evil-minded men bent his bow and shot a shaft at us, but it fell far short of where we sat, and the laugh of those runagates came over the sands to us. So we crept up the beach trembling, and then rose to our feet and got to our horses, and rode hither speedily, and our hearts are broken for thy sorrow."

At that word came Hallblithe's own sister out from the hall; and she bore weapons with her, to wit Hallblithe's sword and shield and helm and hauberk. As for him he turned back silently to his work, and set the steel of the spear on the new ashen shaft, and took the hammer and smote the nail in, and laid the weapon on a round pebble that was thereby, and clenched the nail on the other side. Then he looked

—

about, and saw that the other damsel had brought him his coal-black war-horse ready saddled and bridled; then he did on his armour, and girt his sword to his side and leapt into the saddle, and took his new-shafted spear in hand and shook the rein. But none of all those damsels durst say a word to him or ask him whither he went, for they feared his face, and the sorrow of his heart. So he got him out of the garth and turned toward the sea-shore, and they saw the glitter of his spear-point a minute over the turf-wall, and heard the clatter of his horse-hoofs as he galloped over the hard way; and thus he departed.

# CHAPTER III: THE WARRIORS OF THE RAVEN SEARCH THE SEAS

Then the women bethought them, and they spake a word or two together, and then they sundered and went one this way and one that, to gather together the warriors of the Raven who were a-field, or on the way, nigh unto the house, that they might follow Hallblithe down to the sea-shore and help him; after a while they came back again by one and two and three, bringing with them the wrathful young men; and when there was upward of a score gathered in the garth armed and horsed, they rode their ways to the sea, being minded to thrust a long-ship of the Ravens out over the Rollers into the sea, and follow the strong-thieves of the waters and bring a-back the Hostage, so that they might end the sorrow at once, and establish joy once more in the House of the Raven and the House of the Rose. But they had with them three lads of fifteen winters or thereabouts to lead their horses back home again, when they should have gone up on to the Horse of the Brine.

Thus then they departed, and the maidens stood in the garth-gate till they lost sight of them behind the sandhills, and then turned back sorrowfully into the house, and sat there talking low of their sorrow. And many a time they had to tell their tale anew, as folk came into the hall one after another from field and fell. But the young men came down to the sea, and found Hallblithe's black horse straying about amongst the tamarisk-bushes above the beach; and they looked thence over the sand, and saw neither Hallblithe nor any man: and they gazed out seaward, and saw neither ship nor sail on the barren brine. Then they went down on to the sand, and sundered their fellowship, and went half one way, half the other, betwixt the sandhills and the surf, where now the tide was flowing, till the nesses of the east and the west, the horns of the bay, stayed them. Then they met together again by

—

7

the Rollers, when the sun was within an hour of setting. There and then they laid hand to that ship which is called the Seamew, and they ran her down over the Rollers into the waves, and leapt aboard and hoisted sail, and ran out the oars and put to sea; and a little wind was blowing seaward from the gates of the mountains behind them.

So they quartered the sea-plain, as the kestrel doth the water-meadows, till the night fell on them, and was cloudy, though whiles the wading moon shone out; and they had seen nothing, neither sail nor ship, nor aught else on the barren brine, save the washing of waves and the hovering of sea-fowl. So they lay-to outside the horns of the bay and awaited the dawning. And when morning was come they made way again, and searched the sea, and sailed to the out-skerries, and searched them with care; then they sailed into the main and fared hither and thither and up and down: and this they did for eight days, and in all that time they saw no ship nor sail, save three barks of the Fish-biters nigh to the Skerry which is called Mew-stone.

So they fared home to the Raven Bay, and laid their keel on the Rollers, and so went their ways sadly, home to the House of the Raven: and they deemed that for this time they could do no more in seeking their valiant kinsman and his fair damsel. And they were very sorry; for these two were well-beloved of all men. But since they might not amend it, they abode in peace, awaiting what the change of days might bring them.

# CHAPTER IV: NOW HALLBLITHE TAKETH THE SEA

Now must it be told of Hallblithe that he rode fiercely down to the sea-shore, and from the top of the beach he gazed about him, and there below him was the Ship-stead and Rollers of his kindred, whereon lay the three long-ships, the Seamew, and the Osprey and the Erne. Heavy and huge they seemed to him as they lay there, black-sided, icy-cold with the washing of the March waves, their golden dragon-heads looking seaward wistfully. But first had he looked out into the offing, and it was only when he had let his eyes come back from where the sea and sky met, and they had beheld nothing but the waste of waters, that he beheld the Ship-stead closely; and therewith he saw where a little to the west of it lay a skiff, which the low wave of the tide lifted and let fall from time to time. It had a mast, and a black sail hoisted thereon and flapping with slackened sheet. A man sat in the boat clad in black raiment, and the sun smote a gleam from the helm

—

on his head. Then Hallblithe leapt off his horse, and strode down the sands shouldering his spear; and when he came near to the man in the boat he poised his spear and shook it and cried out: "Man, art thou friend or foe?"

Said the man: "Thou art a fair young man: but there is grief in thy voice along with wrath. Cast not till thou hast heard me, and mayst deem whether I may do aught to heal thy grief."

"What mayst thou do?" said Hallblithe; "art thou not a robber of the sea, a harrier of the folks that dwell in peace?"

The man laughed: "Yea," said he, "my craft is thieving and carrying off the daughters of folk, so that we may have a ransom for them. Wilt thou come over the waters with me?"

Hallblithe said wrathfully:

"Nay, rather, come thou ashore here! Thou seemest a big man, and belike shall be good of thine hands. Come and fight with me; and then he of us who is vanquished, if he be unslain, shall serve the other for a year, and then shalt thou do my business in the ransoming."

The man in the boat laughed again, and that so scornfully that he angered Hallblithe beyond measure: then he arose in the boat and stood on his feet swaying from side to side as he laughed. He was passing big, long-armed and big-headed, and long hair came from under his helm like the tail of a red horse; his eyes were grey and gleaming, and his mouth wide.

In a while he stayed his laughter and said: "O Warrior of the Raven, this were a simple game for thee to play; though it is not far from my mind, for fighting when I needs must win is no dull work. Look you, if I slay or vanquish thee, then all is said; and if by some chance stroke thou slayest me, then is thine only helper in this matter gone from thee. Now to be short, I bid thee come aboard to me if thou wouldst ever hear another word of thy damsel betrothed. And moreover this need not hinder thee to fight with me if thou hast a mind to it thereafter; for we shall soon come to a land big enough for two to stand on. Or if thou listest to fight in a boat rocking on the waves, I see not but there may be manhood in that also."

Now was the hot wrath somewhat run off Hallblithe, nor durst he lose any chance to hear a word of his beloved; so he said: "Big man, I will come aboard. But look thou to it, if thou hast a mind to bewray me; for the sons of the Raven die hard."

"Well," said the big man, "I have heard that their minstrels are of many words, and think that they have tales to tell. Come aboard and

—

loiter not." Then Hallblithe waded the surf and lightly strode over the gunwale of the skiff and sat him down. The big man thrust out into the deep and haled home the sheet; but there was but little wind.

Then said Hallblithe: "Wilt thou have me row, for I wot not whitherward to steer?"

Said the red carle: "Maybe thou art not in a hurry; I am not: do as thou wilt." So Hallblithe took the oars and rowed mightily, while the alien steered, and they went swiftly and lightly over the sea, and the waves were little.

# CHAPTER V: THEY COME UNTO THE ISLE OF RANSOM

So the sun grew low, and it set; the stars and the moon shone a while and then it clouded over. Hallblithe still rowed and rested not, though he was weary; and the big man sat and steered, and held his peace. But when the night was grown old and it was not far from the dawn, the alien said: "Youngling of the Ravens, now shalt thou sleep and I will row."

Hallblithe was exceeding weary; so he gave the oars to the alien and lay down in the stern and slept. And in his sleep he dreamed that he was lying in the House of the Raven, and his sisters came to him and said, "Rise up now, Hallblithe! wilt thou be a sluggard on the day of thy wedding? Come thou with us to the House of the Rose that we may bear away the Hostage." Then he dreamed that they departed, and he arose and clad himself: but when he would have gone out of the hall, then was it no longer daylight, but moonlight, and he dreamed that he had dreamed: nevertheless he would have gone abroad, but might not find the door; so he said he would go out by a window; but the wall was high and smooth (quite other than in the House of the Raven, where were low windows all along one aisle), nor was there any way to come at them. But he dreamed that he was so abashed thereat, and had such a weakness on him, that he wept for pity of himself: and he went to his bed to lie down; and lo! there was no bed and no hall; nought but a heath, wild and wide, and empty under the moon. And still he wept in his dream, and his manhood seemed departed from him, and he heard a voice crying out, "Is this the Land? Is this the Land?"

Therewithal he awoke, and as his eyes cleared he beheld the big man rowing and the black sail flapping against the mast; for the wind had fallen dead and they were faring on over a long smooth swell of the sea. It was broad daylight, but round about them was a thick mist, which seemed none the less as if the sun were ready to shine through it.

As Hallblithe caught the red man's eye, he smiled and nodded on him and said: "Now has the time come for thee first to eat and then to row. But tell me what is that upon thy cheeks?"

Hallblithe, reddening somewhat, said: "The night dew hath fallen on me."

Quoth the sea-rover, "It is no shame for thee a youngling to remember thy betrothed in thy sleep, and to weep because thou lackest her. But now bestir thee, for it is later than thou mayest deem."

Therewith the big man drew in the oars and came to the afterpart of the boat, and drew meat and drink out of a locker thereby; and they ate and drank together, and Hallblithe grew strong and somewhat less downcast; and he went forward and gat the oars into his hands.

Then the big red man stood up and looked over his left shoulder and said: "Soon shall we have a breeze and bright weather."

Then he looked into the midmost of the sail and fell a-whistling such a tune as the fiddles play to dancing men and maids at Yule-tide, and his eyes gleamed and glittered therewithal, and exceeding big he looked. Then Hallblithe felt a little air on his cheek, and the mist grew thinner, and the sail began to fill with wind till the sheet tightened: then, lo! the mist rising from the face of the sea, and the sea's face rippling gaily under a bright sun. Then the wind increased, and the wall of mist departed and a few light clouds sped over the sky, and the sail swelled and the boat heeled over, and the seas fell white from the prow, and they sped fast over the face of the waters.

Then laughed the red-haired man, and said: "O croaker on the dead branch, now is the wind such that no rowing of thine may catch up with it: so in with the oars now, and turn about, and thou shalt see whitherward we are going."

Then Hallblithe turned about on the thwart and looked across the sea, and lo! before them the high cliffs and crags and mountains of a new land which seemed to be an isle, and they were deep blue under the sun, which now shone aloft in the mid heaven. He said nought at all, but sat looking and wondering what land it might be; but the big man said: "O tomb of warriors, is it not as if the blueness of the deep sea had heaved itself up aloft, and turned from coloured air into rock and stone, so wondrous blue it is? But that is because those crags and mountains are so far away, and as we draw nigher to them, thou shalt see them as they verily are, that they are coal-black; and yonder land is an isle, and is called the Isle of Ransom. Therein shall be the market for thee where thou mayst cheapen thy betrothed. There mayst thou take her by the hand and lead her away thence, when thou hast dealt with the chapman of maidens and hast pledged thee by the fowl of battle, and the edge of the fallow blade to pay that which he will have of thee."

As the big man spoke there was a mocking in his voice and his face and in his whole huge body, which made the sword of Hallblithe uneasy in his scabbard; but he refrained his wrath, and said: "Big man, the longer I look, the less I can think how we are to come up on to yonder island; for I can see nought but a huge cliff, and great mountains rising beyond it."

"Thou shalt the more wonder," said the alien, "the nigher thou drawest thereto; for it is not because we are far away that thou canst see no beach or strand, or sloping of the land seaward, but because there is nought of all these things. Yet fear not! am I not with thee? thou shalt come ashore on the Isle of Ransom."

Then Hallblithe held his peace, and the other spake not for a while, but gave a short laugh once or twice; and said at last in a big voice, "Little Carrion-biter, why dost thou not ask me of my name?"

Now Hallblithe was a tall man and a fell fighter; but he said: "Because I was thinking of other things and not of thee."

"Well," said the big man, in a voice still louder, "when I am at home men call me the Puny Fox."

Then Hallblithe said: "Art thou a Fox? It may well be that thou shalt beguile me as such beasts will but look to it, that if thou dost I shall know how to avenge me."

Then rose up the big man from the helm, and straddled wide in the boat, and cried out in a great roaring voice: "Crag-nester, I am one of seven brethren, and the smallest and weakest of them. Art thou not afraid?"

"No," said Hallblithe, "for the six others are not here. Wilt thou fight here in boat, O Fox?"

"Nay," said Fox, "rather we will drink a cup of wine together."

So he opened the locker again and drew out thence a great horn of some huge neat of the outlands, which was girthed and stopped with silver, and also a golden cup, and he filled the cup from the horn and gave it into Hallblithe's hand and said: "Drink, O black-fledged nestling! But call a health over the cup if thou wilt." So Hallblithe raised the cup aloft and cried: "Health to the House of the Raven and to them that love it! an ill day to its foemen!" Then he set his lips to the cup and drank; and that wine seemed to him better and stronger than any he had ever tasted. But when he had given the cup back again to Fox, that red one filled it again, and cried over it, "The Treasure of the Sea! and the King that dieth not!" Then he drank, and filled again for Hallblithe, and steered with his knees meanwhile; and thus they drank three cups each, and Fox smiled and was peaceful and said but little, but Hallblithe sat wondering how the world was changed for him since yesterday.

But now was the sky blown all clear of clouds and the wind piped shrill behind them, and the great waves rose and fell about them, and the sun glittered on them in many colours. Fast flew the boat before the wind as though it would never stop, and the day was waning, and the wind still rising; and now the Isle of Ransom uphove huge before them, and coal-black, and no beach and no haven was to be seen therein; and still they ran before the wind towards that black cliff-wall, against which the sea washed for ever, and no keel ever built by man might live for one moment 'twixt the surf and the cliff of that grim land. The sun grew low, and sank red under the sea, and that world of stone swallowed up half the heavens before them, for they were now come very nigh thereto; nor could Hallblithe see aught for it, but that they must be dashed against the cliff and perish in a moment of time.

Still the boat flew on; but now when the twilight was come, and they had just opened up along reach of the cliff that lay beyond a high ness, Hallblithe thought he saw down by the edge of the sea something darker than the face of the rock-wall, and he deemed it was a cave: they came a little nearer and he saw it was a great cave high enough to let a round-ship go in with all her sails set.

"Son of the Raven," quoth Fox, "hearken, for thy heart is not little. Yonder is the gate into the Isle of Ransom, and if thou wilt, thou mayst go through it. Yet it may be that if thou goest ashore on to the Isle something grievous shall befall thee, a trouble more than thou canst bear: a shame it may be. Now there are two choices for thee: either to go up on to the Isle and face all; or to die here by my hand having done nothing unmanly or shameful: What sayest thou?"

"Thou art of many words when time so presses, Fox," said Hallblithe. "Why should I not choose to go up on to the Island to deliver my trothplight maiden? For the rest, slay me if thou canst, if we come alive out of this cauldron of waters."

Said the big red man: "Look on then, and note Fox how he

---

13

steereth, as it were through a needle's eye."

Now were they underneath the black shadow of the black cliff and amidst the twilight the surf was tossed about like white fire. In the lower heavens the stars were beginning to twinkle and the moon was bright and yellow, and aloft all was peaceful, for no cloud sullied the sky. One moment Hallblithe saw all this hanging above the turmoil of thundering water and dripping rock and the next he was in the darkness of the cave, the roaring wind and the waves still making thunder about him, though of a different voice from the harsh hubbub without. Then he heard Fox say: "Sit down now and take the oars, for presently shall we be at home at the landing place."

So Hallblithe took the oars and rowed, and as they went up the cave the sea fell, and the wind died out into the aimless gustiness of hollow places; and for a little while was all as dark as dark might be. Then Hallblithe saw that the darkness grew a little greyer, and he looked over his shoulder and saw a star of light before the bows of the boat, and Fox cried out: "Yea, it is like day; bright will the moon be for such as needs must be wayfaring to-night! Cease rowing, O Son of the coal-blue fowl, for there is way enough on her."

Then Hallblithe lay on his oars, and in a minute the bows smote the land; then he turned about and saw a steep stair of stone, and up the sloping shaft thereof the moonlit sky and the bright stars. Then Fox arose and came forward and leapt out of the boat and moored her to a big stone: then he leapt back again and said: "Bear a hand with the victuals; we must bring them out of the boat unless thou wilt sleep supperless, as I will not. For to-night must we be guests to ourselves, since it is far to the dwelling of my people, and the old man is said to be a skin-changer, a flit-by-night. And as to this cave, it is deemed to be nowise safe to sleep therein, unless the sleeper have a double share of luck. And thy luck, meseemeth, O Son of the Raven, is as now somewhat less than a single share. So to-night we shall sleep under the naked heaven."

Hallblithe yea-said this, and they took the meat and drink, such as they needed, from out the boat, and climbed the steep stair no little way, and so came out on to a plain place, which seemed to Hallblithe bare and waste so far as he saw it by the moonlight; for the twilight was gone now, and nought was left of the light of day save a glimmer in the west.

This Hallblithe deemed wonderful, that no less out on the open heath and brow of the land than in the shut-in cave, all that tumult of the wind had fallen, and the cloudless night was calm, and with a little air blowing from the south and the landward.

Therewithal was Fox done with his loud-voiced braggart mood, and spoke gently and peaceably like to a wayfarer, who hath business of his to look to as other men. Now he pointed to certain rocks or low crags that a little way off rose like a reef out of the treeless plain; then said he: "Shipmate, underneath yonder rocks is our resting-place for to-night; and I pray thee not to deem me churlish that I give thee no better harbour. But I have a charge over thee to bring thee safe thus far on thy quest; and thou wouldst find it hard to live among such housemates as thou wouldst find up yonder amongst our folks to-night. But to-morrow shalt thou come to speech with him who will deal with thee concerning the ransom."

"It is enough," said Hallblithe, "and I thank thee for thy leading: and as for thy rough and uncomely words which thou hast given me, I pardon thee for them: for I am none the worse of them: forsooth, if I had been, my sword would have had a voice in the matter."

"I am well content as it is, Son of the Raven," quoth Fox; "I have done my bidding and all is well."

"Tell me then who it is hath bidden thee bring me hither?"

"I may not tell thee," said Fox; "thou art here, be content, as I am."

And he spake no more till they had come to the reef aforesaid, which was some two furlongs from the place where they had come from out of the cave. There then they set forth their supper on the stones, and ate what they would, and drank of that good strong wine while the horn bare out. And now was Fox of few words, and when Hallblithe asked him concerning that land, he had little to say. And at last when Hallblithe asked him of that so perilous house and those who manned it, he said to him:

"Son of the Raven, it avails not asking of these matters; for if I tell thee aught concerning them I shall tell thee lies. Once again let it be enough for thee that thou hast passed over the sea safely on thy quest; and a more perilous sea it is forsooth than thou deemest. But now let us have an end of vain words, and make our bed amidst these stones as best we may; for we should be stirring betimes in the morning." Hallblithe said little in answer, and they arrayed their sleeping places cunningly, as the hare doth her form, and like men well used to lying abroad.

Hallblithe was very weary and he soon fell asleep; and as he lay there, he dreamed a dream, or maybe saw a vision; whether he were asleep when he saw it, or between sleeping and waking, I know not. But this was his dream or his vision; that the Hostage was standing over him, and she as he had seen her but yesterday, bright-haired and ruddy-cheeked and white-skinned, kind of hand and soft of voice, and she said to him: "Hallblithe, look on me and hearken, for I have a message for thee." And he looked and longed for her, and his soul was ravished by the sweetness of his longing, and he would have leapt up and cast his arms about her, but sleep and the dream bound him, and he might not. Then the image smiled on him and said: "Nay, my love, lie still, for thou mayst not touch me: here is but the image of the body which thou desirest. Hearken then. I am in evil plight, in the hands of strong-thieves of the sea, nor know I what they will do with me, and I have no will to be shamed; to be sold for a price from one hand to another, yet to be bedded without a price, and to lie beside some foe-man of our folk, and he to cast his arms about me, will I, will I not: this is a hard case. Therefore to-morrow morning at daybreak while men sleep, I think to steal forth to the gunwale of the black ship and give myself to the gods, that they and not these runagates may be masters of my life and my soul, and may do with me as they will: for indeed they know that I may not bear the strange kinless house, and the love and caressing of the alien house-master, and the mocking and stripes of the alien house-mistress. Therefore let the Hoary One of the sea take me and look to my matters, and carry me to life or death, which-so he will. Thin now grows the night, but lie still a little yet, while I speak another word.

"Maybe we shall meet alive again, and maybe not: and if not, though we have never yet lain in one bed together, yet I would have thee remember me: yet not so that my image shall come between thee and thy speech-friend and bed-fellow of the kindred, that shall lie where I was to have lain. Yet again, if I live and thou livest, I have been told and have heard that by one way or other I am like to come to the Glittering Plain, and the Land of Living Men. O my beloved, if by any way thou mightest come thither also, and we might meet there, and we two alive, how good it were! Seek that land then, beloved! seek it, whether or no we once more behold the House of the Rose, or tread the floor of the Raven dwelling. And now must even this image of me sunder from thee. Farewell!"

Therewith was the dream done and the vision departed; and Hallblithe sat up full of anguish and longing; and he looked about him over the dreary land, and it was somewhat light and the sky was grown grey and cloudy, and he deemed that the dawn was come. So he leapt to his feet and stooped down over Fox, and took him by the shoulder, and shook him and said: "Faring-fellow, awake! the dawn is come, and we have much to do."

Fox sat up and growled like a dog, and rubbed his eyes and looked about him and said: "Thou hast waked me for nought: it is the false dawn of the moon that shineth now behind the clouds and casteth no shadow; it is but an hour after midnight. Go to sleep again, and let me be, else will I not be a guide to thee when the day comes." And he lay down and was asleep at once. Then Hallblithe went and lay down again full of sorrow: Yet so weary was he that he presently fell asleep, and dreamed no more.

# CHAPTER VI: OF A DWELLING OF MAN ON THE ISLE OF RANSOM

When he awoke again the sun shone on him, and the morning was calm and windless. He sat up and looked about him, but could see no signs of Fox save the lair wherein he had lain. So he arose to his feet and sought for him about the crannies of the rocks, and found him not; and he shouted for him, and had no answer. Then he said, "Belike he has gone down to the boat to put a thing in, or take a thing out." So he went his ways to the stair down into the water-cave, and he called on Fox from the top of the stair, and had no answer.

So he went down that long stair with a misgiving in his heart, and when he came to the last step there was neither man nor boat, nor aught else save the water and the living rock. Then was he exceeding wroth, for he knew that he had been beguiled, and he was in an evil case, left alone on an Isle that he knew not, a waste and desolate land, where it seemed most like he should die of famine.

He wasted no breath or might now in crying out for Fox, or seeking him; for he said to himself: "I might well have known that he was false and a liar, whereas he could scarce refrain his joy at my folly and his guile. Now is it for me to strive for life against death."

Then he turned and went slowly up the stair, and came out on to the open face of that Isle, and he saw that it was waste indeed, and dreadful: a wilderness of black sand and stones and ice-borne rocks, with here and there a little grass growing in the hollows, and here and there a dreary mire where the white-tufted rushes shook in the wind, and here and there stretches of moss blended with red-blossomed sengreen; and otherwhere nought but the wind-bitten creeping willow clinging to the black sand, with a white bleached stick and a leaf or two, and again a stick and a leaf. In the offing looking landward were great mountains, some very great and snow-capped, some bare to the tops; and all that was far away, save the snow, was deep-blue in the sunny morning. But about him on the heath were scattered rocks like the reef beneath which he had slept the last night, and peaks, and hammers, and knolls of uncouth shapes.

Then he went to the edge of the cliffs and looked down on the sea which lay wrinkled and rippling on toward the shore far below him, and long he gazed thereon and all about, but could see neither ship nor sail, nor aught else save the washing of waves and the hovering of sea fowl.

Then he said: "Were it not well if I were to seek that house-master of whom Fox spake? Might he not flit me at least to the Land of the Glittering Plain? Woe is me! now am I of that woful company, and I also must needs cry out, Where is the land? Where is the land?"

Therewith he turned toward the reef above their lair, but as he went he thought and said: "Nay, but was not this Stead a lie like the rest of Fox's tale? and am I not alone in this sea-girt wilderness? Yea, and even that image of my Beloved which I saw in the dream, perchance that also was a mere beguiling; for now I see that the Puny Fox was in all ways wiser than is meet and comely." Yet again he said: "At least I will seek on, and find out whether there be another man dwelling on this hapless Isle, and then the worst of it will be battle with him, and death by point and edge rather than by hunger; or at the best we may become friends and fellows and deliver each other." Therewith he came to the reef, and with much ado climbed to the topmost of its rocks and looked down thence landward: and betwixt him and the mountains, and by seeming not very far off, he saw smoke arising: but no house he saw, nor any other token of a dwelling. So he came down from the stone and turned his back upon the sea and went toward that smoke with his sword in its sheath, and his spear over his shoulder. Rough and toilsome was the way: three little dales he crossed amidst the mountain necks, each one narrow and bare, with a stream of water amidst, running seaward, and whether in dale or on ridge, he went ever amidst sand and stones, and the weeds of the wilderness, and saw no man, or man-tended beast.

At last, after he had been four hours on the way, but had not gone very far, he topped a stony bent, and from the brow thereof beheld a wide valley grass-grown for the more part, with a river running

---

18

through it, and sheep and kine and horses feeding up and down it. And amidst this dale by the stream-side, was a dwelling of men, a long hall and other houses about it builded of stone.

Then was Hallblithe glad, and he strode down the bent speedily, his war-gear clashing upon him: and as he came to the foot thereof and on to the grass of the dale, he got amongst the pasturing horses, and passed close by the horse-herd and a woman that was with him. They scowled at him as he went by, but meddled not with him in any way. Although they were giant-like of stature and fierce of face, they were not ill-favoured: they were red-haired, and the woman as white as cream where the sun had not burned her skin; they had no weapons that Hallblithe might see save the goad in the hand of the carle.

So Hallblithe passed on and came to the biggest house, the hall aforesaid: it was very long, and low as for its length, not over shapely of fashion, a mere gabled heap of stones. Low and strait was the door thereinto, and as Hallblithe entered stooping lowly, and the fire of the steel of his spear that he held before him was quenched in the mirk of the hall, he smiled and said to himself: "Now if there were one anigh who would not have me enter alive, and he with a weapon in his hand, soon were all the tale told." But he got into the hall unsmitten, and stood on the floor thereof, and spake: "The sele of the day to whomsoever is herein! Will any man speak to the new comer?"

But none answered or gave him greeting; and as his eyes got used to the dusk of the hall, he looked about him, and neither on the floor or the high seat nor in any ingle could he see a man; and there was silence there, save for the crackling of the flickering flame on the hearth amidmost, and the running of the rats behind the panelling of the walls.

On one side of the hall was a row of shut-beds, and Hallblithe deemed that there might be men therein; but since none had greeted him he refrained him from searching them for fear of a trap, and he thought, "I will abide amidst the floor, and if there be any that would deal with me, friend or foe, let him come hither to me."

So he fell to walking up and down the hall from buttery to dais, and his war-gear rattled upon him. At last as he walked he thought he heard a small thin peevish voice, which yet was too husky for the squeak of a rat. So he stayed his walk and stood still, and said: "Will any man speak to Hallblithe, a newcomer, and a stranger in this Stead?"

Then that small voice made a word and said: "Why paceth the fool up and down our hall, doing nothing, even as the Ravens flap croaking about the crags, abiding the war-mote and the clash of the fallow blades?"

Said Hallblithe, and his voice sounded big in the hall: "Who calleth Hallblithe a fool and mocketh at the sons of the Raven?"

Spake the voice: "Why cometh not the fool to the man that may not go to him?"

Then Hallblithe bent forward to hearken, and he deemed that the voice came from one of the shut-beds, so he leaned his spear against a pillar, and went into the shut-bed he had noted, and saw where there lay along in it a man exceeding old by seeming, sore wasted, with long hair as white as snow lying over the bed-clothes.

When the elder saw Hallblithe, he laughed a thin cracked laugh as if in mockery and said: "Hail newcomer! wilt thou eat?"

"Yea," said Hallblithe.

"Go thou into the buttery then," said the old carle, "and there shalt thou find on the cupboard cakes and curds and cheese: eat thy fill, and when thou hast done, look in the ingle, and thou shalt see a cask of mead exceeding good, and a stoup thereby, and two silver cups; fill the stoup and bring it hither with the cups; and then may we talk amidst of drinking, which is good for an old carle. Hasten thou! or I shall deem thee a double fool who will not fare to fetch his meat, though he be hungry."

Then Hallblithe laughed, and went down the hall into the buttery and found the meat, and ate his fill, and came away with the drink back to the Long-hoary man, who chuckled as he came and said: "Fill up now for thee and for me, and call a health to me and wish me somewhat."

"I wish thee luck," said Hallblithe, and drank. Said the elder: "And I wish thee more wits; is luck all that thou mayst wish me? What luck may an outworn elder have?"

"Well then," quoth Hallblithe, "what shall I wish thee? Wouldst thou have me wish thee youth?"

"Yea, certes," said the Long-hoary, "that and nought else."

"Youth then I wish thee, if it may avail thee aught," said Hallblithe, and he drank again therewith.

"Nay, nay," said the old carle peevishly, "take a third cup, and wish me youth with no idle words tacked thereto."

Said Hallblithe raising the cup: "Herewith I wish thee youth!" and he drank.

"Good is the wish," said the elder; "now ask thou the old carle whatso thou wilt."

Said Hallblithe: "What is this land called?"

"Son," said the other, "hast thou heard it called the Isle of Ransom?"

"Yea," said Hallblithe, "but what wilt thou call it?"

"By no other name," said the hoary carle.

"It is far from other lands?" said Hallblithe.

"Yea," said the carle, "when the light winds blow, and the ships sail slow."

"What do ye who live here?" said Hallblithe. "How do ye live, what work win ye?"

"We win diverse work," said the elder, "but the gainfullest is robbing men by the high hand."

"Is it ye who have stolen from me the Hostage of the Rose?" said Hallblithe.

Said the Long-hoary, "Maybe; I wot not; in diverse ways my kinsmen traffic, and they visit many lands. Why should they not have come to Cleveland also?"

"Is she in this Isle, thou old runagate?" said Hallblithe.

"She is not, thou young fool," said the elder. Then Hallblithe flushed red and spake: "Knowest thou the Puny Fox?"

"How should I not?" said the carle, "since he is the son of one of my sons."

"Dost thou call him a liar and a rogue?" said Hallblithe.

The elder laughed; "Else were I a fool," said he; "there are few bigger liars or bigger rogues than the Puny Fox!"

"Is he here in this Isle?" said Hallblithe; "may I see him?"

The old man laughed again, and said: "Nay, he is not here, unless he hath turned fool since yesterday: why should he abide thy sword, since he hath done what he would and brought thee hither?"

Then he laughed, as a hen cackles a long while, and then said: "What more wilt thou ask me?"

But Hallblithe was very wroth: "It availeth nought to ask," he said; "and now I am in two minds whether I shall slay thee or not."

"That were a meet deed for a Raven, but not for a man," said the carle, "and thou that hast wished me luck! Ask, ask!"

But Hallblithe was silent a long while. Then the carle said, "Another cup for the longer after youth!"

Hallblithe filled, and gave to him, and the old man drank and said:

"Thou deemest us all liars in the Isle of Ransom because of thy beguiling by the Puny Fox: but therein thou errest. The Puny Fox is our chiefest liar, and doth for us the more part of such work as we need: therefore, why should we others lie. Ask, ask!"

"Well then," said Hallblithe, "why did the Puny Fox bewray me, and at whose bidding?"

Said the elder: "I know, but I will not tell thee. Is this a lie?"

"Nay, I deem it not," said Hallblithe: "But, tell me, is it verily true that my trothplight is not here, that I may ransom her?"

Said the Long-hoary: "I swear it by the Treasure of the Sea, that she is not here: the tale was but a lie of the Puny Fox."

# CHAPTER VII: A FEAST IN THE ISLE OF RANSOM

Hallblithe pondered his answer awhile with downcast eyes and said at last: "Have ye a mind to ransom me, now that I have walked into the trap?"

"There is no need to talk of ransom," said the elder; "thou mayst go out of this house when thou wilt, nor will any meddle with thee if thou strayest about the Isle, when I have set a mark on thee and given thee a token: nor wilt thou be hindered if thou hast a mind to leave the Isle, if thou canst find means thereto; moreover as long as thou art in the Isle, in this house mayst thou abide, eating and drinking and resting with us."

"How then may I leave this Isle?" said Hallblithe.

The elder laughed: "In a ship," said he.

"And when," said Hallblithe, "shall I find a ship that shall carry me?"

Said the old carle, "Whither wouldest thou my son?" Hallblithe was silent a while, thinking what answer he should make; then he said: "I would go to the land of the Glittering Plain."

"Son, a ship shall not be lacking thee for that voyage," said the elder. "Thou mayst go to-morrow morn. And I bid thee abide here to-night, and thy cheer shall not be ill. Yet if thou wilt believe my word, it will be well for thee to say as little as thou mayst to any man here, and that little as little proud as maybe: for our folk are short of temper and thou knowest there is no might against many. Indeed it is not unlike that they will not speak one word to thee, and if that be so, thou hast no need to open thy mouth to them. And now I will tell thee that it is good that thou hast chosen to go to the Glittering Plain. For if thou wert otherwise minded, I wot not how thou wouldest get thee a keel to carry thee, and the wings have not yet begun to sprout on thy shoulders, raven though thou be. Now I am glad that thou art going thy ways to the Glittering Plain to-morrow; for thou wilt be good company to me on the way: and I deem that thou wilt be no churl when thou art glad."

"What," said Hallblithe, "art thou wending thither, thou old man?"

"Yea," said he, "nor shall any other be on the ship save thou and I, and the mariners that waft us; and they forsooth shall not go aland there. Why should not I go, since there are men to bear me aboard?"

Said Hallblithe, "And when thou art come aland there, what wilt thou do?"

"Thou shalt see, my son," said the Long-hoary. "It may be that thy good wishes shall be of avail to me. But now since all this may only be if I live through this night, and since my heart hath been warmed by the good mead, and thy fellowship, and whereas I am somewhat sleepy, and it is long past noon, go forth into the hall, and leave me to sleep, that I may be as sound as eld will let me to-morrow. And as for thee, folk, both men and women, shall presently come into the hall, and I deem not that any shall meddle with thee; but if so be that any challenge thee, whatsoever may be his words, answer thou to him, 'The House of the Undying,' and there will be an end of it. Only look thou to it that no naked steel cometh out of thy scabbard. Go now, and if thou wilt, go out of doors; yet art thou safer within doors and nigher unto me."

So Hallblithe went back into the main hall, and the sun had gotten round now, and was shining into the hall, through the clerestory windows, so that he saw clearly all that was therein. And he deemed the hall fairer within than without; and especially over the shut-beds were many stories carven in the panelling, and Hallblithe beheld them gladly. But of one thing he marvelled, that whereas he was in an island of the strong-thieves of the waters, and in their very home and chiefest habitation, there were no ships or seas pictured in that imagery, but fair groves and gardens, with flowery grass and fruited trees all about. And there were fair women abiding therein, and lovely young men, and warriors, and strange beasts and many marvels, and the ending of wrath and beginning of pleasure and the crowning of love. And amidst these was pictured oft and again a mighty king with a sword by his side and a crown on his head; and ever was he smiling and joyous, so that Hallblithe, when he looked on him, felt of better heart and smiled back on the carven image.

So while Hallblithe looked on these things, and pondered his case carefully, all alone as he was in that alien hall, he heard a noise without of talking and laughter, and presently the pattering of feet therewith, and then women came into the hall, a score or more, some young, some old, some fair enough, and some hard-featured and uncomely, but all above the stature of the women whom he had seen in his own land.

So he stood amidst the hall-floor and abided them; and they saw him and his shining war-gear, and ceased their talking and laughter, and drew round about him, and gazed at him; but none said aught till an old crone came forth from the ring, and said "Who art thou, standing under weapons in our hall?"

He knew not what to answer, and held his peace; and she spake again: "Whither wouldest thou, what seekest thou?"

Then answered Hallblithe: "The House of the Undying."

None answered, and the other women all fell away from him at once, and went about their business hither and thither through the hall. But the old crone took him by the hand, and led him up to the dais, and set him next to the midmost high-seat. Then she made as if she would do off his war-gear, and he would not gainsay her, though he deemed that foes might be anear; for in sooth he trusted in the old carle that he would not bewray him, and moreover he deemed it would be unmanly not to take the risks of the guesting, according to the custom of that country.

So she took his armour and his weapons and bore them off to a shut-bed next to that wherein lay the ancient man, and she laid the gear within it, all save the spear, which she laid on the wall-pins above; and she made signs to him that therein he was to lie; but she spake no word to him. Then she brought him the hand-washing water in a basin of latten, and a goodly towel therewith, and when he had washed she went away from him, but not far.

This while the other women were busy about the hall; some swept the floor down, and when it was swept strawed thereon rushes and handfuls of wild thyme: some went into the buttery and bore forth the boards and the trestles: some went to the chests and brought out the rich hangings, the goodly bankers and dorsars, and did them on the walls: some bore in the stoups and horns and beakers, and some went their ways and came not back a while, for they were busied about the cooking. But whatever they did, none hailed him, or heeded him more

24

than if he had been an image, as he sat there looking on. None save the old woman who brought him the fore-supper, to wit a great horn of mead, and cakes and dried fish.

So was the hall arrayed for the feast very fairly, and Hallblithe sat there while the sun westered and the house grew dim, and dark at last, and they lighted the candles up and down the hall. But a little after these were lit, a great horn was winded close without, and thereafter came the clatter of arms about the door, and exceeding tall weaponed men came in, one score and five, and strode two by two up to the foot of the dais, and stood there in a row. And Hallblithe deemed their war-gear exceeding good; they were all clad in ring-locked byrnies, and had steel helms on their heads with garlands of gold wrought about them and they bore spears in their hands, and white shields hung at their backs. Now came the women to them and unarmed them; and under their armour their raiment was black; but they had gold rings on their arms, and golden collars about their necks. So they strode up to the dais and took their places on the high-seat, not heeding Hallblithe any more than if he were an image of wood. Nevertheless that man sat next to him who was the chieftain of all and sat in the midmost high-seat; and he bore his sheathed sword in his hand and laid it on the board before him, and he was the only man of those chieftains who had a weapon.

But when these were set down there was again a noise without, and there came in a throng of men armed and unarmed who took their places on the end-long benches up and down the hall; with these came women also, who most of them sat amongst the men, but some busied them with the serving: all these men were great of stature, but none so big as the chieftains on the high-seat.

Now came the women in from the kitchen bearing the meat, whereof no little was flesh-meat, and all was of the best. Hallblithe was duly served like the others, but still none spake to him or even looked on him; though amongst themselves they spoke in big, rough voices so that the rafters of the hall rang again.

When they had eaten their fill the women filled round the cups and the horns to them, and those vessels were both great and goodly. But ere they fell to drinking uprose the chieftain who sat furthest from the midmost high-seat on the right and cried a health: "The Treasure of the Sea!" Then they all stood up and shouted, women as well as men, and emptied their horns and cups to that health. Then stood up the man furthest on the left and cried out, "Drink a health to the Undying

King!" And again all men rose up and shouted ere they drank. Other healths they drank, as the "Cold Keel," the "Windworn Sail," the "Quivering Ash" and the "Furrowed Beach." And the wine and mead flowed like rivers in that hall of the Wild Men. As for Hallblithe, he drank what he would but stood not up, nor raised his cup to his lips when a health was drunk; for he knew not whether these men were his friends or his foes, and he deemed it would be little-minded to drink to their healths, lest he might be drinking death and confusion to his own kindred.

But when men had drunk a while, again a horn blew at the nether end of the hall, and straightway folk arose from the endlong tables, and took away the boards and trestles, and cleared the floor and stood against the wall; then the big chieftain beside Hallblithe arose and cried out: "Now let man dance with maid, and be we merry! Music, strike up!" Then flew the fiddle-bows and twanged the harps, and the carles and queens stood forth on the floor; and all the women were clad in black raiment, albeit embroidered with knots and wreaths of flowers. A while they danced and then suddenly the music fell, and they all went back to their places. Then the chieftain in the high-seat arose and took a horn from his side, and blew a great blast on it that filled the hall; then he cried in a loud voice: "Be we merry! Let the champions come forth!"

Men shouted gleefully thereat, and straightway ran into the hall from out the screens three tall men clad all in black armour with naked swords in their hands, and stood amidst the hall-floor, somewhat on one side, and clashed their swords on their shields and cried out: "Come forth ye Champions of the Raven!"

Then leapt Hallblithe from his seat and set his hand to his left side, but no sword was there; so he sat down again, remembering the warning of the Elder, and none heeded him.

Then there came into the hall slowly and mournfully three men-at-arms, clad and weaponed like the warriors of his folk, with the image of the Raven on their helms and shields. So Hallblithe refrained him, for besides that this seemed like to be a fair battle of three against three, he doubted some snare, and he determined to look on and abide.

So the champions fell to laying on strokes that were no child's play, though Hallblithe doubted if the edges bit, and it was but a little while before the Champions of the Raven fell one after another before the Wild Men, and folk drew them by the heels out into the buttery. Then

---

26

arose great laughter and jeering, and exceeding wroth was Hallblithe; howbeit he refrained him because he remembered all he had to do. But the three Champions of the Sea strode round the hall, tossing up their swords and catching them as they fell, while the horns blew up behind them.

After a while the hall grew hushed, and the chieftain arose and cried: "Bring in now some sheaves of the harvest we win, we lads of the oar and the arrow!" Then was there a stir at the screen doors, and folk pressed forward to see, and, lo, there came forward a string of women, led in by two weaponed carles; and the women were a score in number, and they were barefoot and their hair hung loose and their gowns were ungirt, and they were chained together wrist to wrist; yet had they gold at arm and neck: there was silence in the hall when they stood amidst of the floor.

Then indeed Hallblithe could not refrain himself, and he leapt from his seat and on to the board, and over it, and ran down the hall, and came to those women and looked them in the face one by one, while no man spake in the hall. But the Hostage was not amongst them; nay forsooth, they none of them favoured of the daughters of his people, though they were comely and fair; so that again Hallblithe doubted if this were aught but a feast-hall play done to anger him; whereas there was but little grief in the faces of those damsels, and more than one of them smiled wantonly in his face as he looked on them.

So he turned about and went back to his seat, having said no word, and behind him arose much mocking and jeering; but it angered him little now; for he remembered the rede of the elder and how that he had done according to his bidding, so that he deemed the gain was his. So sprang up talk in the hall betwixt man and man, and folk drank about and were merry, till the chieftain arose again and smote the board with the flat of his sword, and cried out in a loud and angry voice, so that all could hear: "Now let there be music and minstrelsy ere we wend bedward!"

Therewith fell the hubbub of voices, and there came forth three men with great harps, and a fourth man with them, who was the minstrel; and the harpers smote their harps so that the roof rang therewith, and the noise, though it was great, was tuneable, and when they had played thus a little while, they abated their loudness somewhat, and the minstrel lifted his voice and sang:

The land lies black     With winter's lack,     The wind blows cold     Round field and fold;     All folk are within,     And but weaving they win.Where from finger to finger the shuttle flies fast,And the eyes of the singer look fain on the cast,As he singeth the story of summer undoneAnd the barley sheaves hoary ripe under the sun.

Then the maidens stay     The light-hung sley,     And the shuttles bide     By the blue web's side,     While hand in hand With the carles they stand.But ere to the measure the fiddles strike up,And the elders yet treasure the last of the cup,There stand they a-hearkening the blast from the lift,And e'en night is a-darkening more under the drift.

There safe in the hall     They bless the wall,     And the roof o'er head,     Of the valiant stead;     And the hands they praise     Of the olden days.Then through the storm's roaring the fiddles break out,And they think not of warring, but cast away doubt,And, man before maiden, their feet tread the floor,And their hearts are unladen of all that they bore.

But what winds are o'er-cold     For the heart of the bold? What seas are o'er-high     For the undoomed to die?     Dark night and dread wind,     But the haven we find.Then ashore mid the flurry of stone-washing surf!Cloud-hounds the moon worry, but light lies the turf;Lo the long dale before us! the lights at the end,Though the night darkens o'er us, bid whither to wend.

Who beateth the door     By the foot-smitten floor?     What guests are these     From over the seas?     Take shield and sword For their greeting-word.Lo, lo, the dance ended! Lo, midst of the hallThe fallow blades blended! Lo, blood on the wall!Who liveth, who dieth? O men of the sea,For peace the folk crieth; our masters are ye.

Now the dale lies grey     At the dawn of day;     And fair feet

pass    O'er the wind-worn grass;    And they turn back to gaze
On the roof of old days.Come tread ye the oaken-floored hall of the
sea!Be your hearts yet unbroken; so fair as ye be,That kings are
abiding unwedded to gainThe news of our riding the steeds of the
main.

Much shouting and laughter arose at the song's end; and men
sprang up and waved their swords above the cups, while Hallblithe sat
scowling down on their merriment. Lastly arose the chieftain and
called out loudly for the good-night cup, and it went round and all
men drank. Then the horn blew for bed, and the chieftains went to
their chambers, and the others went to the out-bowers or laid them
down on the hall-floor, and in a little while none stood upright
thereon. So Hallblithe arose, and went to the shut-bed appointed for
him, and laid him down and slept dreamlessly till the morning.

# CHAPTER VIII: HALLBLITHE TAKETH SHIP AGAIN AWAY FROM THE ISLE OF RANSOM

When he awoke, the sun shone into the hall by the windows above
the buttery, and there were but few folk left therein. But so soon as
Hallblithe was clad, the old woman came to him, and took him by the
hand, and led him to the board, and signed to him to eat of what was
thereon; and he did so; and by then he was done, came folk who went
into the shut-bed where lay the Long-hoary, and they brought him
forth bed and all and bare him out a-doors. Then the crone brought
Hallblithe his arms and he did on byrny and helm, girt his sword to his
side, took his spear in his hand and went out a-doors; and there close
by the porch lay the Long-hoary upon a horse-litter. So Hallblithe
came up to him and gave him the sele of the day: and the elder said:
"Good morrow, son, I am glad to see thee. Did they try thee hard last
night?"

And Hallblithe saw two of the carles that had borne out the elder,
that they were talking together, and they looked on him and laughed
mockingly; so he said to the elder: "Even fools may try a wise man, and
so it befell last night. Yet, as thou seest, mumming hath not slain me."

Said the old man: "What thou sawest was not all mumming; it was
done according to our customs; and well nigh all of it had been done,
even hadst thou not been there. Nay, I will tell thee; at some of our

feasts it is not lawful to eat either for the chieftains or the carles, till a champion hath given forth a challenge, and been answered and met, and the battle fought to an end. But ye men, what hindereth you to go to the horses' heads and speed on the road the chieftain who is no longer way-worthy?"

So they ran to the horses and set down the dale by the riverside, and just as Hallblithe was going to follow afoot, there came a swain from behind the house leading a red horse which he brought to Hallblithe as one who bids mount. So Hallblithe leapt into the saddle and at once caught up with the litter of the Long-hoary down along the river. They passed by no other house, save here and there a cot beside some fold or byre; they went easily, for the way was smooth by the river-side; so in less than two hours they came where the said river ran into the sea. There was no beach there, for the water was ten fathom deep close up to the lip of the land; but there was a great haven land-locked all but a narrow outgate betwixt the sheer black cliffs. Many a great ship might have lain in that haven; but as now there was but one lying there, a round-ship not very great, but exceeding trim and meet for the sea.

There without more ado the carles took the elder from the litter and bore him aboard, and Hallblithe followed him as if he had been so appointed. They laid the old man adown on the poop under a tilt of precious web, and so went aback by the way that they had come; and Hallblithe went and sat down beside the Long-hoary, who spake to him and said: "Seest thou, son, how easy it is for us twain to be shipped for the land whither we would go? But as easy as it is for thee to go thither whereas we are going, just so hard had it been for thee to go elsewhere. Moreover I must tell thee that though many an one of the Isle of Ransom desireth to go this voyage, there shall none else go, till the world is a year older, and he who shall go then shall be likest to me in all ways, both in eld and in feebleness, and in gibing speech, and all else; and now that I am gone, his name shall be the same as that whereby ye may call me to-day, and that is Grandfather. Art thou glad or sorry, Hallblithe?"

"Grandfather," said Hallblithe, "I can scarce tell thee: I move as one who hath no will to wend one way or other. Meseems I am drawn to go thither whereas we are going; therefore I deem that I shall find my beloved on the Glittering Plain: and whatever befalleth afterward, let it be as it will!"

"Tell me, my son," said the Grandfather, "how many women are there in the world?"

"How may I tell thee?" said Hallblithe.

"Well, then," said the elder, "how many exceeding fair women are there?"

Said Hallblithe, "Indeed I wot not."

"How many of such hast thou seen?" said the Grandfather.

"Many," said Hallblithe; "the daughters of my folk are fair, and there will be many other such amongst the aliens."

Then laughed the elder, and said: "Yet, my son, he who had been thy fellow since thy sundering from thy beloved, would have said that in thy deeming there is but one woman in the world; or at least one fair woman: is it not so?"

Then Hallblithe reddened at first, as though he were angry; then he said: "Yea, it is so."

Said the Grandfather in a musing way: "I wonder if before long I shall think of it as thou dost."

Then Hallblithe gazed at him marvelling, and studied to see wherein lay the gibe against himself; and the Grandfather beheld him, and laughed as well as he might, and said: "Son, son; didst thou not wish me youth?"

"Yea," said Hallblithe, "but what ails thee to laugh so? What is it I have said or done?"

"Nought, nought," said the elder, laughing still more, "only thou lookest so mazed. And who knoweth what thy wish may bring forth?"

Thereat was Hallblithe sore puzzled; but while he set himself to consider what the old carle might mean, uprose the hale and how of the mariners; they cast off the hawsers from the shore, ran out the sweeps, and drave the ship through the haven-gates. It was a bright sunny day; within, the green water was oily-smooth, without the rippling waves danced merrily under a light breeze, and Hallblithe deemed the wind to be fair; for the mariners shouted joyously and made all sail on the ship; and she lay over and sped through the waves, casting off the seas from her black bows. Soon were they clear of those swart cliffs, and it was but a little afterwards that the Isle of Ransom was grown deep blue behind them and far away.

# CHAPTER IX: THEY COME TO THE LAND OF THE GLITTERING PLAIN

As in the hall, so in the ship, Hallblithe noted that the folk were merry and of many words one with another, while to him no man cast a word save the Grandfather. As to Hallblithe, though he wondered much what all this betokened, and what the land was whereto he was wending, he was no man to fear an unboded peril; and he said to himself that whatever else betid, he should meet the Hostage on the Glittering Plain; so his heart rose and he was of good cheer, and as the Grandfather had foretold, he was a merry faring-fellow to him. Many a gibe the old man cast at him, and whiles Hallblithe gave him back as good as he took, and whiles he laughed as the stroke went home and silenced him; and whiles he understood nought of what the elder said. So wore the day and still the wind held fair, though it was light; and the sun set in a sky nigh cloudless, and there was nowhere any forecast of peril. But when night was come, Hallblithe lay down on a fair bed, which was dight for him in the poop, and he soon fell asleep and dreamed not save such dreams as are but made up of bygone memories, and betoken nought, and are not remembered.

When he awoke, day lay broad on the sea, and the waves were little, the sky had but few clouds, the sun shone bright, and the air was warm and sweet-breathed.

He looked aside and saw the old man sitting up in his bed, as ghastly as a dead man dug up again: his bushy eyebrows were wrinkled over his bleared old eyes, the long white hair dangled forlorn from his gaunt head: yet was his face smiling and he looked as happy as the soul within him could make the half-dead body. He turned now to Hallblithe and said:

"Thou art late awake: hadst thou been waking earlier, the sooner had thine heart been gladdened. Go forward now, and gaze thy fill and come and tell me thereof."

"Thou art happy, Grandfather," said Hallblithe, "what good tidings hath morn brought us?"

"The Land! the Land!" said the Long-hoary; "there are no longer tears in this old body, else should I be weeping for joy."

Said Hallblithe: "Art thou going to meet some one who shall make thee glad before thou diest, old man?"

"Some one?" said the elder; "what one? Are they not all gone? burned, and drowned, and slain and died abed? Some one, young man? Yea, forsooth some one indeed! Yea, the great warrior of the Wasters of the Shore; the Sea-eagle who bore the sword and the torch and the terror of the Ravagers over the coal-blue sea. It is myself, Myself that I shall find on the Land of the Glittering Plain, O young lover!"

Hallblithe looked on him wondering as he raised his wasted arms towards the bows of the ship pitching down the slope of the sunlit sea, or climbing up it. Then again the old man fell back on his bed and muttered: "What fool's work is this! that thou wilt draw me on to talk loud, and waste my body with lack of patience. I will talk with thee no more, lest my heart swell and break, and quench the little spark of life within me."

Then Hallblithe arose to his feet, and stood looking at him, wondering so much at his words, that for a while he forgat the land which they were nearing, though he had caught glimpses of it, as the bows of the round-ship fell downward into the hollow of the sea. The wind was but light, as hath been said, and the waves little under it, but there was still a smooth swell of the sea which came of breezes now dead, and the ship wallowed thereon and sailed but slowly.

In a while the old man opened his eyes again, and said in a low peevish voice: "Why standest thou staring at me? why hast thou not gone forward to look upon the land? True it is that ye Ravens are short of wits."

Said Hallblithe: "Be not wrath, chieftain; I was wondering at thy words, which are exceeding marvellous; tell me more of this land of the Glittering Plain."

Said the Grandfather: "Why should I tell it thee? ask of the mariners. They all know more than thou dost."

"Thou knowest," said Hallblithe, "that these men speak not to me, and take no more heed of me than if I were an image which they were carrying to sell to the next mighty man they may hap on. Or tell me, thou old man," said he fiercely, "is it perchance a thrall-market whereto they are bringing me? Have they sold her there, and will they sell me also in the same place, but into other hands."

"Tush!" said the Grandfather somewhat feebly, "this last word of thine is folly; there is no buying or selling in the land whereto we are bound. As to thine other word, that these men have no fellowship with thee, it is true: thou art my fellow and the fellow of none else aboard. Therefore if I feel might in me, maybe I will tell thee somewhat."

Then he raised his head a little and said: "The sun grows hot, the wind faileth us, and slow and slow are we sailing."

Even as he spoke there was a stir amidships, and Hallblithe looked and beheld the mariners handling the sweeps, and settling themselves on the rowing-benches. Said the elder: "There is noise amidships, what are they doing?"

---

33

The old man raised himself a little again, and cried out in his shrill voice: "Good lads! brave lads! Thus would we do in the old time when we drew anear some shore, and the beacons were sending up smoke by day, and flame benights; and the shore-abiders did on their helms and trembled. Thrust her through, lads! Thrust her along!" Then he fell back again, and said in a weak voice: "Make no more delay, guest, but go forward and look upon the land, and come back and tell me thereof, and then the tale may flow from me. Haste, haste!" So Hallblithe went down from the poop, and in to the waist, where now the rowers were bending to their oars, and crying out fiercely as they tugged at the quivering ash; and he clomb on to the forecastle and went forward right to the dragon-head, and gazed long upon the land, while the dashing of the oar-blades made the semblance of a gale about the ship's black sides. Then he came back again to the Sea-eagle, who said to him: "Son, what hast thou seen?"

"Right ahead lieth the land, and it is still a good way off. High rise the mountains there, but by seeming there is no snow on them; and though they be blue they are not blue like the mountains of the Isle of Ransom. Also it seemed to me as if fair slopes of woodland and meadow come down to the edge of the sea. But it is yet far away."

"Yea," said the elder, "is it so? Then will I not wear myself with making words for thee. I will rest rather, and gather might. Come again when an hour hath worn, and tell me what thou seest; and may happen then thou shalt have my tale!" And he laid him down therewith and seemed to be asleep at once. And Hallblithe might not amend it; so he waited patiently till the hour had worn, and then went forward again, and looked long and carefully, and came back and said to the Sea-eagle, "The hour is worn."

The old chieftain turned himself about and said "What hast thou seen?"

Said Hallblithe: "The mountains are pale and high, and below them are hills dark with wood, and betwixt them and the sea is a fair space of meadowland, and methought it was wide."

Said the old man: "Sawest thou a rocky skerry rising high out of the sea anigh the shore?"

"Nay," said Hallblithe, "if there be, it is all blended with the meadows and the hills."

Said the Sea-eagle: "Abide the wearing of another hour, and come and tell me again, and then I may have a gainful word for thee." And he fell asleep again. But Hallblithe abided, and when the hour was worn, he went forward and stood on the forecastle. And this was the third shift of the rowers, and the stoutest men in the ship now held the oars in their hands, and the ship shook through all her length and breadth as they drave her over the waters.

So Hallblithe came aft to the old man and found him asleep; so he took him by the shoulder, and shook him and said: "Awake, faring-fellow, for the land is a-nigh."

So the old man sat up and said: "What hast thou seen?"

Said Hallblithe: "I have seen the peaks and cliffs of the far-off mountains; and below them are hills green with grass and dark with woods, and thence stretch soft green meadows down to the sea-strand, which is fair and smooth, and yellow."

"Sawest thou the skerry?" said the Sea-eagle.

"Yea, I saw it," said Hallblithe, "and it rises sheer from out the sea about a mile from the yellow strand; but its rocks are black, like the rocks of the Isle of Ransom."

"Son," said the elder, "give me thine hands and raise me up a little." So Hallblithe took him and raised him up, so that he sat leaning against the pillows; and he looked not on Hallblithe, but on the bows of the ship, which now pitched but a little up and down, for the sea was laid quiet now. Then he cried in his shrill, piping voice: "It is the Land! It is the Land!"

But after a little while he turned to Hallblithe and spake: "Short is the tale to tell: thou hast wished me youth, and thy wish hath thriven; for to-day, ere the sun goes down, thou shalt see me as I was in the days when I reaped the harvest of the sea with sharp sword and hardy heart. For this is the land of the Undying King, who is our lord and our gift-giver; and to some he giveth the gift of youth renewed, and life that shall abide here the Gloom of the Gods. But none of us all may come to the Glittering Plain and the King Undying without turning the back for the last time on the Isle of Ransom: nor may any men of the Isle come hither save those who are of the House of the Sea-eagle, and few of those, save the chieftains of the House, such as are they who sat by thee on the high-seat that even. Of these once in a while is chosen one of us, who is old and spent and past battle, and is borne to this land and the gift of the Undying. Forsooth some of us have no will to take the gift, for they say they are liefer to go to where they shall meet more of our kindred than dwell on the Glittering Plain and the Acre of the Undying; but as for me I was ever an overbearing and masterful man, and meseemeth it is well that I meet as few of our kindred as may be: for they are a strifeful race."

Hereat Hallblithe marvelled exceedingly, and he said: "And what am I in all this story? Why am I come hither with thy furtherance?"

Said the Sea-eagle: "We had a charge from the Undying King concerning thee, that we should bring thee hither alive and well, if so be thou camest to the Isle of Ransom. For what cause we had the charge, I know not, nor do I greatly heed."

Said Hallblithe: "And shall I also have that gift of undying youth, and life while the world of men and gods endureth?"

"I must needs deem so," said the Sea-eagle, "so long as thou abidest on the Glittering Plain; and I see not how thou mayst ever escape thence."

Now Hallblithe heard him, how he said "escape," and thereat he was somewhat ill at ease, and stood and pondered a little. At last he said: "Is this then all that thou hast to tell me concerning the Glittering Plain?"

"By the Treasure of the Sea!" said the elder, "I know no more of it. The living shall learn. But I suppose that thou mayst seek thy troth-plight maiden there all thou wilt. Or thou mayst pray the Undying King to have her thither to thee. What know I? At least, it is like that there shall be no lack of fair women there: or else the promise of youth renewed is nought and vain. Shall this not be enough for thee?"

"Nay," said Hallblithe.

"What," said the elder, "must it be one woman only?"

"One only," said Hallblithe.

The old man laughed his thin mocking laugh, and said: "I will not assure thee but that the land of the Glittering Plain shall change all that for thee so soon as it touches the soles of thy feet."

Hallblithe looked at him steadily and smiled, and said: "Well is it then that I shall find the Hostage there; for then shall we be of one mind, either to sunder or to cleave together. It is well with me this day."

"And with me it shall be well ere long," said the Sea-eagle.

But now the rowers ceased rowing and lay on their oars, and the shipmen cast anchor; for they were but a bowshot from the shore, and the ship swung with the tide and lay side-long to the shore. Then said the Sea-eagle: "Look forth, shipmate, and tell me of the land."

And Hallblithe looked and said: "The yellow beach is sandy and shell-strewn, as I deem, and there is no great space of it betwixt the sea and the flowery grass; and a bowshot from the strand I see a little wood amidst which are fair trees blossoming."

"Seest thou any folk on the shore?" said the old man. "Yea," said Hallblithe, "close to the edge of the sea go four; and by seeming three are women, for their long gowns flutter in the wind. And one of these is clad in saffron colour, and another in white, and another in watchet; but the carle is clad in dark red; and their raiment is all glistening as with gold and gems; and by seeming they are looking at our ship as though they expected somewhat."

Said the Sea-eagle: "Why now do the shipmen tarry and have not made ready the skiff? Swillers and belly-gods they be; slothful swine that forget their chieftain."

But even as he spake came four of the shipmen, and without more ado took him up, bed and all, and bore him down into the waist of the ship, whereunder lay the skiff with four strong rowers lying on their oars. These men made no sign to Hallblithe, nor took any heed of him; but he caught up his spear, and followed them and stood by as they lowered the old man into the boat. Then he set his foot on the gunwale of the ship and leapt down lightly into the boat, and none hindered or helped him; and he stood upright in the boat, a goodly image of battle with the sun flashing back from his bright helm, his spear in his hand, his white shield at his back, and thereon the image of the Raven; but if he had been but a salt-boiling carle of the sea-side none would have heeded him less.

# CHAPTER X: THEY HOLD CONVERSE WITH FOLK OF THE GLITTERING PLAIN

Now the rowers lifted the ash-blades, and fell to rowing towards shore: and almost with the first of their strokes, the Sea-eagle moaned out:

"Would we were there, oh, would we were there! Cold groweth eld about my heart. Raven's Son, thou art standing up; tell me if thou canst see what these folk of the land are doing, and if any others have come thither?"

Said Hallblithe: "There are none others come, but kine and horses are feeding down the meadows. As to what those four are doing, the women are putting off their shoon, and girding up their raiment, as if they would wade the water toward us; and the carle, who was barefoot before, wendeth straight towards the sea, and there he standeth, for very little are the waves become."

The old man answered nothing, and did but groan for lack of patience; but presently when the water was yet waist deep the rowers stayed the skiff, and two of them slipped over the gunwale into the sea, and between them all they took up the chieftain on his bed and got him forth from the boat and went toward the strand with him; and the landsfolk met them where the water was shallower, and took him from their hands and bore him forth on to the yellow sand, and laid him down out of reach of the creeping ripple of the tide. Hallblithe withal slipped lightly out of the boat and waded the water after them. But the shipmen rowed back again to their ship, and presently Hallblithe heard the hale and how, as they got up their anchor.

But when Hallblithe was come ashore, and was drawn near the folk of the land, the women looked at him askance, and they laughed and said: "Welcome to thee also, O young man!" And he beheld them, and saw that they were of the stature of the maidens of his own land; they were exceeding fair of skin and shapely of fashion, so that the nakedness of their limbs under their girded gowns, and all glistening with the sea, was most lovely and dainty to behold. But Hallblithe knelt by the Sea-eagle to note how he fared, and said: "How is it with thee, O chieftain?"

The old man answered not a word, and he seemed to be asleep, and Hallblithe deemed that his cheeks were ruddier and his skin less wasted and wrinkled than aforetime. Then spake one of those women: "Fear not, young man; he is well and will soon be better." Her voice was as sweet as a spring bird in the morning; she was white-skinned and dark-haired, and full sweetly fashioned; and she laughed on Hallblithe, but not mockingly; and her fellows also laughed, as though it was strange for him to be there. Then they did on their shoon again, and with the carle laid their hands to the bed whereon the old man lay, and lifted him up, and bore him forth on to the grass, turning their faces toward the flowery wood aforesaid; and they went a little way and then laid him down again and rested; and so on little by little, till they had brought him to the edge of the wood, and still he seemed to be asleep. Then the damsel who had spoken before, she with the dark hair, said to Hallblithe, "Although we have gazed on thee as if with wonder, this is not because we did not look to meet thee, but because thou art so fair and goodly a man: so abide thou here till we come back to thee from out of the wood."

Therewith she stroked his hand, and with her fellows lifted the old man once more, and they bore him out of sight into the thicket.

But Hallblithe went to and fro a dozen paces from the wood, and looked across the flowery meads and deemed he had never seen any so fair. And afar off toward the hills he saw a great roof arising, and thought he could see men also; and nigher to him were kine pasturing, and horses also, whereof some drew anear him and stretched out their necks and gazed at him; and they were goodly after their kind; and a fair stream of water came round the corner out of the wood and down the meadows to the sea; and Hallblithe went thereto and could see that there was but little ebb and flow of the tide on that shore; for the water of the stream was clear as glass, and the grass and flowers grew right down to its water; so he put off his helm and drank of the stream and washed his face and his hands therein, and then did on his helm again and turned back again toward the wood, feeling very strong and merry; and he looked out seaward and saw the Ship of the Isle of Ransom lessening fast; for a little land wind had arisen and they had spread their sails to it; and he laid down on the grass till the four folk of the country came out of the wood again, after they had been gone somewhat less than an hour, but the Sea-eagle was not with them: and Hallblithe rose up and turned to them, and the carle saluted him and departed, going straight toward that far-away roof he had seen; and the women were left with Hallblithe, and they looked at him and he at them as he stood leaning on his spear.

Then said the black-haired damsel: "True it is, O Spearman, that if we did not know of thee, our wonder would be great that a man so young and lucky-looking should have sought hither."

"I wot not why thou shouldest wonder," said Hallblithe; "I will tell thee presently wherefore I come hither. But tell me, is this the Land of the Glittering Plain?"

"Even so," said the damsel, "dost thou not see how the sun shineth on it? Just so it shineth in the season that other folks call winter."

"Some such marvel I thought to hear of," said he; "for I have been told that the land is marvellous; and fair though these meadows be, they are not marvellous to look on now: they are like other lands, though it maybe, fairer."

"That may be," she said; "we have nought but hearsay of other lands. If we ever knew them we have forgotten them."

Said Hallblithe, "Is this land called also the Acre of the Undying?"

As he spake the words the smile faded from the damsel's face; she and her fellows grew pale, and she said: "Hold thy peace of such words! They are not lawful for any man to utter here. Yet mayst thou call it the Land of the Living."

He said: "I crave pardon for the rash word."

Then they smiled again, and drew near to him, and caressed him with their hands, and looked on him lovingly; but he drew a little aback from them and said: "I have come hither seeking something which I have lost, the lack whereof grieveth me."

Quoth the damsel, drawing nearer to him again, "Mayst thou find it, thou lovely man, and whatsoever else thou desirest."

Then he said: "Hath a woman named the Hostage been brought hither of late days? A fair woman, bright-haired and grey-eyed, kind of countenance, soft of speech, yet outspoken and nought timorous; tall according to our stature, but very goodly of fashion; a woman of the House of the Rose, and my troth-plight maiden."

They looked on each other and shook their heads, and the black-haired damsel spake: "We know of no such a woman, nor of the kindred which thou namest."

Then his countenance fell, and became piteous with desire and grief, and he bent his brows upon them, for they seemed to him light-minded and careless, though they were lovely.

But they shrank from him trembling, and drew aback; for they had all been standing close to him, beholding him with love, and she who had spoken most had been holding his left hand fondly. But now she said: "Nay, look not on us so bitterly! If the woman be not in the land, this cometh not of our malice. Yet maybe she is here. For such as come hither keep not their old names, and soon forget them what they were. Thou shalt go with us to the King, and he shall do for thee what thou wilt; for he is exceeding mighty."

Then was Hallblithe appeased somewhat; and he said: "Are there many women in the land?"

"Yea, many," said that damsel.

"And many that are as fair as ye be?" said he. Then they laughed and were glad, and drew near to him again and took his hands and kissed them; and the black-haired damsel said: "Yea, yea, there be many as fair as we be, and some fairer," and she laughed.

"And that King of yours," said he, "how do ye name him?"

"He is the King," said the damsel.

"Hath he no other name?" said Hallblithe.

"We may not utter it," she said; "but thou shalt see him soon, that there is nought but good in him and mightiness."

# CHAPTER XI: THE SEA-EAGLE

# RENEWETH HIS LIFE

But while they spake together thus, came a man from out of the wood very tall of stature, red-bearded and black-haired, ruddy-cheeked, full-limbed, most joyous of aspect; a man by seeming of five and thirty winters. He strode straight up to Hallblithe, and cast his arms about him, and kissed his cheek, as if he had been an old and dear friend newly come from over seas.

Hallblithe wondered and laughed, and said: "Who art thou that deemest me so dear?"

Said the man: "Short is thy memory, Son of the Raven, that thou in so little space hast forgotten thy shipmate and thy faring-fellow; who gave thee meat and drink and good rede in the Hall of the Ravagers." Therewith he laughed joyously and turned about to the three maidens and took them by the hands and kissed their lips, while they fawned upon him lovingly.

Then said Hallblithe: "Hast thou verily gotten thy youth again, which thou badest me wish thee?"

"Yea, in good sooth," said the red-bearded man; "I am the Sea-eagle of old days; and I have gotten my youth, and love therewithal, and somewhat to love moreover."

Therewith he turned to the fairest of the damsels, and she was white-skinned and fragrant as the lily, rose-cheeked and slender, and the wind played with the long locks of her golden hair, which hung down below her knees; so he cast his arms about her and strained her to his bosom, and kissed her face many times, and she nothing loth, but caressing him with lips and hand. But the other two damsels stood by smiling and joyous: and they clapped their hands together and kissed each other for joy of the new lover; and at last fell to dancing and skipping about them like young lambs in the meadows of Spring-tide. But amongst them all, stood up Hallblithe leaning on his spear with smiling lips and knitted brow; for he was pondering in his mind in what wise he might further his quest.

But after they had danced a while the Sea-eagle left his love that he had chosen and took a hand of either of the two damsels, and led them tripping up to Hallblithe, and cried out: "Choose thou, Raven's baby, which of these twain thou wilt have to thy mate; for scarcely shalt thou see better or fairer."

But Hallblithe looked on them proudly and sternly, and the black-haired damsel hung down her head before him and said softly: "Nay, nay, sea-warrior; this one is too lovely to be our mate. Sweeter love abides him, and lips more longed for."

Then stirred Hallblithe's heart within him and he said: "O Eagle of the Sea, thou hast thy youth again: what then wilt thou do with it? Wilt thou not weary for the moonlit main, and the washing of waves and the dashing of spray, and thy fellows all glistening with the brine? Where now shall be the alien shores before thee, and the landing for fame, and departure for the gain of goods? Wilt thou forget the ship's black side, and the dripping of the windward oars, as the squall falleth on when the sun hath arisen, and the sail tuggeth hard on the sheet, and the ship lieth over and the lads shout against the whistle of the wind? Has the spear fallen from thine hand, and hast thou buried the sword of thy fathers in the grave from which thy body hath escaped? What art thou, O Warrior, in the land of the alien and the King? Who shall heed thee or tell the tale of thy glory, which thou hast covered over with the hand of a light woman, whom thy kindred knoweth not, and who was not born in a house wherefrom it hath been appointed thee from of old to take the pleasure of woman? Whose thrall art thou now, thou lifter of the spoil, thou scarer of the freeborn? The bidding of what lord or King wilt thou do, O Chieftain, that thou mayst eat thy meat in the morning and lie soft in thy bed in the evening?"

"O Warrior of the Ravagers, here stand I, Hallblithe of the Raven, and I am come into an alien land beset with marvels to seek mine own, and find that which is dearest to mine heart; to wit, my troth-plight maiden the Hostage of the Rose, the fair woman who shall lie in my bed, and bear me children, and stand by me in field and fold, by thwart and gunwale, before the bow and the spear, by the flickering of the cooking-fire, and amidst the blaze of the burning hall, and beside the bale-fire of the warrior of the Raven. O Sea-eagle, my guester amongst the foemen, my fellow-farer and shipmate, say now once for all whether thou wilt help me in my quest, or fall off from me as a dastard?"

Again the maidens shrank before his clear and high-raised voice, and they trembled and grew pale.

But the Sea-eagle laughed from a countenance kind with joy, and said: "Child of the Raven, thy words are good and manly: but it availeth nought in this land, and I wot not how thou wilt fare, or why thou hast been sent amongst us. What wilt thou do? Hadst thou spoken these words to the Long-hoary, the Grandfather, yesterday, his ears would have been deaf to them; and now that thou speakest them to the Sea-eagle, this joyous man on the Glittering Plain, he cannot do according to them, for there is no other land than this which can hold him. Here he is strong and stark, and full of joy and love; but otherwhere he would be but a gibbering ghost drifting down the wind of night. Therefore in whatsoever thou mayst do within this land I will stand by thee and help thee; but not one inch beyond it may my foot go, whether it be down into the brine of the sea, or up into the clefts of the mountains which are the wall of this goodly land.

"Thou hast been my shipmate and I love thee, I am thy friend; but here in this land must needs be the love and the friendship. For no ghost can love thee, no ghost may help thee. And as to what thou sayest concerning the days gone past and our joys upon the tumbling sea, true it is that those days were good and lovely; but they are dead and gone like the lads who sat on the thwart beside us, and the maidens who took our hands in the hall to lead us to the chamber. Other days have come in their stead, and other friends shall cherish us. What then? Shall we wound the living to pleasure the dead, who cannot heed it? Shall we curse the Yuletide, and cast foul water on the Holy Hearth of the winter feast, because the summer once was fair and the days flit and the times change? Now let us be glad! For life liveth."

Therewith he turned about to his damsel and kissed her on the mouth. But Hallblithe's face was grown sad and stern, and he spake slowly and heavily: "So is it, shipmate, that whereas thou sayest that the days flit, for thee they shall flit no more; and the day may come for thee when thou shalt be weary, and know it, and long for the lost which thou hast forgotten. But hereof it availeth nought for me to speak any longer, for thine ears are deaf to these words, and thou wilt not hear them. Therefore I say no more save that I thank thee for thy help whatsoever it may be; and I will take it, for the day's work lieth before me, and I begin to think that it may be heavy enough."

The women yet looked downcast, and as if they would be gone out of earshot; but the Sea-eagle laughed as one who is well content, and said: "Thou thyself wilt make it hard for thyself after the wont of thy proud and haughty race; but for me nothing is hard any longer; neither thy scorn nor thy forebodings of evil. Be thou my friend as much as thou canst, and I will be thine wholly. Now ye women, whither will ye lead us? For I am ready to see any new thing ye will show us."

Said his damsel: "We will take you to the King, that your hearts may be the more gladdened. And as for thy friend the Spearman, O Sea-warrior, let not his heart be downcast. Who wotteth but that these

---

two desires, the desire of his heart, and the desire of a heart for him, may not be one and the same desire, so that he shall be fully satisfied?" As she spoke she looked sidelong at Hallblithe, with shy and wheedling eyes; and he wondered at her word, and a new hope sprang up in his heart that he was presently to be brought face to face with the Hostage, and that this was that love, sweeter than their love, which abode in him, and his heart became lighter, and his visage cleared.

# CHAPTER XII: THEY LOOK ON THE KING OF THE GLITTERING PLAIN

So now the women led them along up the stream, and Hallblithe went side by side by the Sea-eagle; but the women had become altogether merry again, and played and ran about them as gamesome as young goats; and they waded the shallows of the clear bright stream barefoot to wash their limbs of the sea-brine, and strayed about the meadows, plucking the flowers and making them wreaths and chaplets, which they did upon themselves and the Sea-eagle; but Hallblithe they touched not, for still they feared him. They went on as the stream led them up toward the hills, and ever were the meads about them as fair and flowery as might be. Folk they saw afar off, but fell in with none for a good while, saving a man and a maid clad lightly as for mid-summer days, who were wandering together lovingly and happily by the stream-side, and who gazed wonderingly on the stark Sea-eagle, and on Hallblithe with his glittering spear. The black-haired damsel greeted these twain and spake something to them, and they laughed merrily, and the man stooped down amongst the grasses and blossoms of the bank, and drew forth a basket, and spread dainty victuals on the grass under a willow-tree, and bade them be his guests that fair afternoon. So they sat down there above the glistering stream and ate and drank and were merry. Thereafter the new-comers and their way-leaders departed with kind words, and still set their faces towards the hills.

At last they saw before them a little wooded hill, and underneath it something red and shining, and other coloured things gleaming in the sun about it. Then said the Sea-eagle: "What have we yonder?"

Said his damsel: "That is the pavilion of the King; and about it are the tents and tilts of our folk who are of his fellowship: for oft he abideth in the fields with them, though he hath houses and halls as fair as the heart of man can conceive."

"Hath he no foemen to fear?" said the Sea-eagle.

"How should that be?" said the damsel. "If perchance any came into this land to bring war upon him, their battle-anger should depart when once the bliss of the Glittering Plain had entered into their souls, and they would ask for nought but leave to abide here and be happy. Yet I trow that if he had foemen he could crush them as easily as I set my foot on this daisy."

So as they went on they fell in with many folk, men and women, sporting and playing in the fields; and there was no semblance of eld on any of them, and no scar or blemish or feebleness of body or sadness of countenance; nor did any bear a weapon or any piece of armour. Now some of them gathered about the new-corners, and wondered at Hallblithe and his long spear and shining helm and dark grey byrny; but none asked concerning them, for all knew that they were folk new come to the bliss of the Glittering Plain. So they passed amidst these fair folk little hindered by them, and into Hallblithe's thoughts it came how joyous the fellowship of such should be and how his heart should be raised by the sight of them, if only his troth-plight maiden were by his side.

Thus then they came to the King's pavilion, where it stood in a bight of the meadow-land at the foot of the hill, with the wood about it on three sides. So fair a house Hallblithe deemed he had never seen; for it was wrought all over with histories and flowers, and with hems sewn with gold, and with orphreys of gold and pearl and gems.

There in the door of it sat the King of the Land in an ivory chair; he was clad in golden gown, girt with a girdle of gems, and had his crown on his head and his sword by his side. For this was the hour wherein he heard what any of his folk would say to him, and for that very end he sat there in the door of his tent, and folk were standing before him, and sitting and lying on the grass round about; and now one, now another, came up to him and spoke before him.

His face shone like a star; it was exceeding beauteous, and as kind as the even of May in the gardens of the happy, when the scent of the eglantine fills all the air. When he spoke his voice was so sweet that all hearts were ravished, and none might gainsay him.

But when Hallblithe set eyes on him, he knew at once that this was he whose carven image he had seen in the Hall of the Ravagers, and his heart beat fast, and he said to himself: "Hold up thine head now, O Son of the Raven, strengthen thine heart, and let no man or god cow thee. For how can thine heart change, which bade thee go to the house wherefrom it was due to thee to take the pleasure of woman, and there to pledge thy faith and troth to her that loveth thee most, and hankereth for thee day by day and hour by hour, so that great is the love that we twain have builded up."

Now they drew nigh, for folk fell back before them to the right and left, as before men who are new come and have much to do; so that there was nought between them and the face of the King. But he smiled upon them so that he cheered their hearts with the hope of fulfilment of their desires, and he said: "Welcome, children! Who be these whom ye have brought hither for the increase of our joy? Who is this tall, ruddy-faced, joyous man so meet for the bliss of the Glittering Plain? And who is this goodly and lovely young man, who beareth weapons amidst our peace, and whose face is sad and stern beneath the gleaming of his helm?"

Said the dark-haired damsel: "O King! O Gift-giver and assurer of joy! this tall one is he who was once oppressed by eld, and who hath come hither to thee from the Isle of Ransom, according to the custom of the land."

Said the King: "Tall man, it is well that thou art come. Now are thy days changed and thou yet alive. For thee battle is ended, and therewith the reward of battle, which the warrior remembereth not amidst the hard hand-play: peace hath begun, and thou needest not be careful for the endurance thereof: for in this land no man hath a lack which he may not satisfy without taking aught from any other. I deem not that thine heart may conceive a desire which I shall not fulfil for thee, or crave a gift which I shall not give thee."

Then the Sea-eagle laughed for joy, and turned his head this way and that, so that he might the better take to him the smiles of all those that stood around.

Then the King said to Hallblithe: "Thou also art welcome; I know thee who thou art: meseemeth great joy awaiteth thee, and I will fulfil thy desire to the uttermost."

Said Hallblithe: "O great King of a happy land, I ask of thee nought save that which none shall withhold from me uncursed."

"I will give it to thee," said the King, "and thou shalt bless me. But what is it which thou wouldst? What more canst thou have than the Gifts of the land?"

Said Hallblithe: "I came hither seeking no gifts, but to have mine own again; and that is the bodily love of my troth-plight maiden. They stole her from me, and me from her; for she loved me. I went down to the sea-side and found her not, nor the ship which had borne her away. I sailed from thence to the Isle of Ransom, for they told me that there I should buy her for a price; neither was her body there. But her image came to me in a dream of the night, and bade me seek to her hither. Therefore, O King, if she be here in the land, show me how I shall find her, and if she be not here, show me how I may depart to seek her otherwhere. This is all my asking."

Said the King: "Thy desire shall be satisfied; thou shalt have the woman who would have thee, and whom thou shouldst have."

Hallblithe was gladdened beyond measure by that word; and now did the King seem to him a comfort and a solace to every heart, even as he had deemed of his carven image in the Hall of the Ravagers; and he thanked him, and blessed him.

But the King bade him abide by him that night, and feast with him. "And on the morrow," said he, "thou shalt go thy ways to look on her whom thou oughtest to love."

Therewith was come the eventide and beginning of night, warm and fragrant and bright with the twinkling of stars, and they went into the King's pavilion, and there was the feast as fair and dainty as might be; and Hallblithe had meat from the King's own dish, and drink from his cup; but the meat had no savour to him and the drink no delight, because of the longing that possessed him.

And when the feast was done, the damsels led Hallblithe to his bed in a fair tent strewn with gold about his head like the starry night, and he lay down and slept for sheer weariness of body.

# CHAPTER XIII: HALLBLITHE BEHOLDETH THE WOMAN WHO LOVETH HIM

But on the morrow the men arose, and the Sea-eagle and his damsel came to Hallblithe; for the other two damsels were departed, and the Sea-eagle said to him:

"Here am I well honoured and measurelessly happy; and I have a message for thee from the King."

"What is it?" said Hallblithe; but he deemed that he knew what it would be, and he reddened for the joy of his assured hope.

Said the Sea-eagle: "Joy to thee, O shipmate! I am to take thee to the place where thy beloved abideth, and there shalt thou see her, but not so as she can see thee; and thereafter shalt thou go to the King, that thou mayst tell him if she shall accomplish thy desire."

Then was Hallblithe glad beyond measure, and his heart danced within him, and he deemed it but meet that the others should be so joyous and blithe with him, for they led him along without any delay, and were glad at his rejoicing; and words failed him to tell of his gladness.

But as he went, the thoughts of his coming converse with his beloved curled sweetly round his heart, so that scarce anything had seemed so sweet to him before; and he fell a-pondering what they twain, he and the Hostage, should do when they came together again; whether they should abide on the Glittering Plain, or go back again to Cleveland by the Sea and dwell in the House of the Kindred; and for his part he yearned to behold the roof of his fathers and to tread the meadow which his scythe had swept, and the acres where his hook had smitten the wheat. But he said to himself, "I will wait till I hear her desire hereon."

Now they went into the wood at the back of the King's pavilion and through it, and so over the hill, and beyond it came into a land of hills and dales exceeding fair and lovely; and a river wound about the dales, lapping in turn the feet of one hill-side or the other; and in each dale (for they passed through two) was a goodly house of men, and tillage about it, and vineyards and orchards. They went all day till the sun was near setting, and were not weary, for they turned into the houses by the way when they would, and had good welcome and meat and drink and what they would of the folk that dwelt there. Thus anigh sunset they came into a dale fairer than either of the others, and nigh to the end where they had entered it was an exceeding goodly house. Then said the damsel:

"We are nigh-hand to our journey's end; let us sit down on the grass by this river-side whilst I tell thee the tale which the King would have thee know."

So they sat down on the grass beside the brimming river, scant two bowshots from that fair house, and the damsel said, reading from a scroll which she drew from her bosom:

"O Spearman, in yonder house dwelleth the woman foredoomed to love thee: if thou wouldst see her, go thitherward, following the path which turneth from the river-side by yonder oak-tree, and thou shalt presently come to a thicket of bay-trees at the edge of an apple-orchard, whose trees are blossoming; abide thou hidden by the bay-leaves, and thou shalt see maidens come into the orchard, and at last one fairer than all the others. This shall be thy love fore-doomed, and none other; and thou shalt know her by this token, that when she hath set her down on the grass beside the bay-tree, she shall say to her maidens 'Bring me now the book wherein is the image of my beloved, that I may solace myself with beholding it before the sun goes down and the night cometh.'"

Now Hallblithe was troubled when she read out these words, and he said: "What is this tale about a book? I know not of any book that lieth betwixt me and my beloved."

"O Spearman," said the damsel, "I may tell thee no more, because I know no more. But keep up thine heart! For dost thou know any more than I do what hath befallen thy beloved since thou wert sundered from her? and why should not this matter of the book be one of the things that hath befallen her? Go now with joy, and come again blessing us."

"Yea, go, faring-fellow," said the Sea-eagle, "and come back joyful, that we may all be merry together. And we will abide thee here."

Hallblithe foreboded evil, but he held his peace and went his ways down the path by the oak-tree; and they abode there by the water-side, and were very merry talking of this and that (but no whit of Hallblithe), and kissing and caressing each other; so that it seemed but a little while to them ere they saw Hallblithe coming back by the oak-tree. He went slowly, hanging his head like a man sore-burdened with grief: thus he came up to them, and stood there above them as they lay on the fragrant grass, and he saying no word and looking so sad and sorry, and withal so fell, that they feared his grief and his anger, and would fain have been away from him; so that they durst not ask him a question for a long while, and the sun sank below the hill while they abided thus.

Then all trembling the damsel spake to the Sea-eagle: "Speak to him, dear friend, else must I flee away, for I fear his silence."

Quoth the Sea-eagle: "Shipmate and friend, what hath betided? How art thou? May we hearken, and mayhappen amend it?"

Then Hallblithe cast himself adown on the grass and said: "I am accursed and beguiled; and I wander round and round in a tangle that I may not escape from. I am not far from deeming that this is a land of dreams made for my beguiling. Or has the earth become so full of lies, that there is no room amidst them for a true man to stand upon his feet and go his ways?"

Said the Sea-eagle: "Thou shalt tell us of what hath betid, and so ease the sorrow of thy soul if thou wilt. Or if thou wilt, thou shalt nurse thy sorrow in thine heart and tell no man. Do what thou wilt;

am I not become thy friend?"

Said Hallblithe: "I will tell you twain the tidings, and thereafter ask me no more concerning them. Hearken. I went whereas ye bade me, and hid myself in the bay-tree thicket; and there came maidens into the blossoming orchard and made a resting-place with silken cushions close to where I was lurking, and stood about as though they were looking for some one to come. In a little time came two more maidens, and betwixt them one so much fairer than any there, that my heart sank within me: whereas I deemed because of her fairness that this would be the fore-doomed love whereof ye spake, and lo, she was in nought like to my troth-plight maiden, save that she was exceeding beauteous: nevertheless, heart-sick as I was, I determined to abide the token that ye told me of. So she lay down amidst those cushions, and I beheld her that she was sad of countenance; and she was so near to me that I could see the tears welling into her eyes, and running down her cheeks; so that I should have grieved sorely for her had I not been grieving so sorely for myself. For presently she sat up and said 'O maiden, bring me hither the book wherein is the image of my beloved, that I may behold it in this season of sunset wherein I first beheld it; that I may fill my heart with the sight thereof before the sun is gone and the dark night come.'

"Then indeed my heart died within me when I wotted that this was the love whereof the King spake, that he would give to me, and she not mine own beloved, yet I could not choose but abide and look on a while, and she being one that any man might love beyond measure. Now a maiden went away into the house and came back again with a book covered with gold set with gems; and the fair woman took it and opened it, and I was so near to her that I saw every leaf clearly as she turned the leaves. And in that book were pictures of many things, as flaming mountains, and castles of war, and ships upon the sea, but chiefly of fair women, and queens, and warriors and kings; and it was done in gold and azure and cinnabar and minium. So she turned the leaves, till she came to one whereon was pictured none other than myself, and over against me was the image of mine own beloved, the Hostage of the Rose, as if she were alive, so that the heart within me swelled with the sobbing which I must needs refrain, which grieved me like a sword-stroke. Shame also took hold of me as the fair woman spoke to my painted image, and I lying well-nigh within touch of her hand; but she said: 'O my beloved, why dost thou delay to come to me? For I deemed that this eve at least thou wouldst come, so many and strong as are the meshes of love which we have cast about thy feet. Oh come to-morrow at the least and latest, or what shall I do, and wherewith shall I quench the grief of my heart? Or else why am I the daughter of the Undying King, the Lord of the Treasure of the Sea? Why have they wrought new marvels for me, and compelled the Ravagers of the Coasts to serve me, and sent false dreams flitting on the wings of the night? Yea, why is the earth fair and fruitful, and the heavens kind above it, if thou comest not to-night, nor to-morrow, nor the day after? And I the daughter of the Undying, on whom the days shall grow and grow as the grains of sand which the wind heaps up above the sea-beach. And life shall grow huger and more hideous round about the lonely one, like the ling-worm laid upon the gold, that waxeth thereby, till it lies all around about the house of the queen entrapped, the moveless unending ring of the years that change not.'

"So she spake till the weeping ended her words, and I was all abashed with shame and pale with anguish. I stole quietly from my lair unheeded of any, save that one damsel said that a rabbit ran in the hedge, and another that a blackbird stirred in the thicket. Behold me, then, that my quest beginneth again amidst the tangle of lies whereinto I have been entrapped."

# CHAPTER XIV: HALLBLITHE HAS SPEECH WITH THE KING AGAIN

He stood up when he had made an end, as a man ready for the road; but they lay there downcast and abashed, and had no words to answer him. For the Sea-eagle was sorry that his faring-fellow was hapless, and was sorry that he was sorry; and as for the damsel, she had not known but that she was leading the goodly Spearman to the fulfilment of his heart's desire. Albeit after a while she spake again and said:

"Dear friends, day is gone and night is at hand; now to-night it were ill lodging at yonder house; and the next house on our backward road is over far for wayworn folk. But hard by through the thicket is a fair little wood-lawn, by the lip of a pool in the stream wherein we may bathe us to-morrow morning; and it is grassy and flowery and sheltered from all winds that blow, and I have victual enough in my wallet. Let us sup and rest there under the bare heaven, as oft is the wont of us in this land; and on the morrow early we will arise and get us back again to Wood-end, where yet the King abideth, and there shalt thou talk to him again, O Spearman."

---

Said Hallblithe: "Take me whither ye will; but now nought availeth. I am a captive in a land of lies, and here most like shall I live betrayed and die hapless."

"Hold thy peace, dear friend, of such words as those last," said she, "or I must needs flee from thee, for they hurt me sorely. Come now to this pleasant place."

She took him by the hand and looked kindly on him, and the Sea-eagle followed him, murmuring an old song of the harvest-field, and they went together by a path through a thicket of white-thorn till they came unto a grassy place. There then they sat them down, and ate and drank what they would, sitting by the lip of the pool till a waning moon was bright over their heads. And Hallblithe made no semblance of content; but the Sea-eagle and his damsel were grown merry again, and talked and sang together like autumn stares, with the kissing and caressing of lovers.

So at last those twain lay down amongst the flowers, and slept in each other's arms; but Hallblithe betook him to the brake a little aloof, and lay down, but slept not till morning was at hand, when slumber and confused dreams overtook him.

He was awaked from his sleep by the damsel, who came pushing through the thicket all fresh and rosy from the river, and roused him, and said:

"Awake now, Spearman, that we may take our pleasure in the sun; for he is high in the heavens now, and all the land laughs beneath him."

Her eyes glittered as she spoke, and her limbs moved under her raiment as though she would presently fall to dancing for very joy. But Hallblithe arose wearily, and gave her back no smile in answer, but thrust through the thicket to the water, and washed the night from off him, and so came back to the twain as they sat dallying together over their breakfast. He would not sit down by them, but ate a morsel of bread as he stood, and said: "Tell me how I can soonest find the King: I bid you not lead me thither, but let me go my ways alone. For with me time presses, and with you meseemeth time is nought. Neither am I a meet fellow for the happy."

But the Sea-eagle sprang up, and swore with a great oath that he would nowise leave his shipmate in the lurch. And the damsel said: "Fair man, I had best go with thee; I shall not hinder thee, but further thee rather, so that thou shalt make one day's journey of two."

And she put forth her hand to him, and caressed him smiling, and fawned upon him, and he heeded it little, but hung not aback from them since they were ready for the road: so they set forth all three together.

They made such diligence on the backward road that the sun was not set by then they came to Wood-end; and there was the King sitting in the door of his pavilion. Thither went Hallblithe straight, and thrust through the throng, and stood before the King; who greeted him kindly, and was no less sweet of face than on that other day.

Hallblithe hailed him not, but said: "King, look on my anguish, and if thou art other than a king of dreams and lies, play no longer with me, but tell me straight out if thou knowest of my troth-plight maiden, whether she is in this land or not."

Then the King smiled on him and said: "True it is that I know of her; yet know I not whether she is in this land or not."

"King," said Hallblithe, "wilt thou bring us together and stay my heart's bleeding?"

Said the King: "I cannot, since I know not where she is."

"Why didst thou lie to me the other day?" said Hallblithe.

"I lied not," said the King; "I bade bring thee to the woman that loved thee, and whom thou shouldst love; and that is my daughter. And look thou! Even as I may not bring thee to thine earthly love, so couldst thou not make thyself manifest before my daughter, and become her deathless love. Is it not enough?"

He spake sternly for all that he smiled, and Hallblithe said: "O King, have pity on me!"

"Yea," said the King; "pity thee I do: but I will live despite thy sorrow; my pity of thee shall not slay me, or make thee happy. Even in such wise didst thou pity my daughter."

Said Hallblithe: "Thou art mighty, O King, and maybe the mightiest. Wilt thou not help me?"

"How can I help thee?" said the King, "thou who wilt not help thyself. Thou hast seen what thou shouldst do: do it then and be holpen."

Then said Hallblithe: "Wilt thou not slay me, O King, since thou wilt not do aught else?"

"Nay," said the King, "thy slaying wilt not serve me nor mine: I will neither help nor hinder. Thou art free to seek thy love wheresoever thou wilt in this my realm. Depart in peace!"

Hallblithe saw that the King was angry, though he smiled upon him; yet so coldly, that the face of him froze the very marrow of

Hallblithe's bones: and he said within himself: "This King of lies shall not slay me, though mine anguish be hard to bear: for I am alive, and it may be that my love is in this land, and I may find her here, and how to reach another land I know not."

So he turned from before the face of the King as the sun was setting, and he went down the land southward betwixt the mountains and the sea, not heeding whether it were night or day; and he went on till it was long past midnight, and then for mere weariness laid him down under a tree, not knowing where he was, and fell asleep.

And in the morning he woke up to the bright sun, and found folk standing round about him, both men and women, and their sheep were anigh them, for they were shepherd folk. So when they saw that he was awake, they greeted him, and were blithe with him and made much of him: and they took him home to their house, and gave him to eat and to drink, and asked him what he would that they might serve him. And they seemed to him to be kind and simple folk, and though he loathed to speak the words, so sick at heart he was, yet he told them how he was seeking his troth-plight maiden, his earthly love, and asked them to say if they had seen any woman like her.

They heard him kindly and pitied him, and told him how they had heard of a woman in the land, who sought her beloved even as he sought his. And when he heard that, his heart leapt up, and he asked them to tell him more concerning this woman. Then they said that she dwelt in the hill-country in a goodly house, and had set her heart on a lovely man, whose image she had seen in a book, and that no man but this one would content her; and this, they said, was a sad and sorry matter, such as was unheard of hitherto in the land.

So when Hallblithe heard this, as heavily as his heart fell again, he changed not countenance, but thanked the kind folk and departed, and went on down the land betwixt the mountains and the sea, and before nightfall he had been into three more houses of folk, and asked there of all comers concerning a woman who was sundered from her beloved; and at none of them gat he any answer to make him less sorry than yesterday. At the last of the three he slept, and on the morrow early there was the work to begin again; and the next day was the same as the last, and the day after differed not from it. Thus he went on seeking his beloved betwixt the mountains and the plain, till the great rock-wall came down to the side of the sea and made an end of the Glittering Plain on that side. Then he turned about and went back by the way he had come, and up the country betwixt the mountains and the plain northward, until he had been into every house of folk in those parts and asked his question.

Then he went up into that fair country of the dales, and even anigh to where dwelt the King's Daughter, and otherwhere in the land and everywhere, quartering the realm of the Glittering Plain as the heron quarters the flooded meadow when the waters draw aback into the river. So that now all people knew him when he came, and they wondered at him; but when he came to any house for the third or fourth time, they wearied of him, and were glad when he departed.

Ever it was one of two answers that he had: either folk said to him, "There is no such woman; this land is happy, and nought but happy people dwell herein;" or else they told him of the woman who lived in sorrow, and was ever looking on a book, that she might bring to her the man whom she desired.

Whiles he wearied and longed for death, but would not die until there was no corner of the land unsearched. Whiles he shook off weariness, and went about his quest as a craftsman sets about his work in the morning. Whiles it irked him to see the soft and merry folk of the land, who had no skill to help him, and he longed for the house of his fathers and the men of the spear and the plough; and thought, "Oh, if I might but get me back, if it were but for an hour and to die there, to the meadows of the Raven, and the acres beneath the mountains of Cleveland by the Sea. Then at least should I learn some tale of what is or what hath been, howsoever evil the tidings were, and not be bandied about by lies for ever."

# CHAPTER XV: YET HALLBLITHE SPEAKETH WITH THE KING

So wore the days and the moons; and now were some six moons worn since first he came to the Glittering Plain; and he was come to Wood-end again, and heard and knew that the King was sitting once more in the door of his pavilion to hearken to the words of his people, and he said to himself: "I will speak yet again to this man, if indeed he be a man; yea, though he turn me into stone."

And he went up toward the pavilion; and on the way it came into his mind what the men of the kindred were doing that morning; and he had a vision of them as it were, and saw them yoking the oxen to the plough, and slowly going down the acres, as the shining iron drew the long furrow down the stubble-land, and the light haze hung about the elm-trees in the calm morning, and the smoke rose straight into the air from the roof of the kindred. And he said: "What is this? am I death-doomed this morning that this sight cometh so clearly upon me amidst the falseness of this unchanging land?"

Thus he came to the pavilion, and folk fell back before him to the right and the left, and he stood before the King, and said to him: "I cannot find her; she is not in thy land."

Then spake the King, smiling upon him, as erst: "What wilt thou then? Is it not time to rest?"

He said: "Yea, O King; but not in this land."

Said the King: "Where else than in this land wilt thou find rest? Without is battle and famine, longing unsatisfied, and heart-burning and fear; within it is plenty and peace and good will and pleasure without cease. Thy word hath no meaning to me."

Said Hallblithe: "Give me leave to depart, and I will bless thee."

"Is there nought else to do?" said the King.

"Nought else," said Hallblithe.

Therewith he felt that the King's face changed though he still smiled on him, and again he felt his heart grow cold before the King.

But the King spake and said: "I hinder not thy departure, nor will any of my folk. No hand will be raised against thee; there is no weapon in all the land, save the deedless sword by my side and the weapons which thou bearest."

Said Hallblithe: "Dost thou not owe me a joy in return for my beguiling?"

"Yea," said the King, "reach out thine hand to take it."

"One thing only may I take of thee," said Hallblithe; "my troth-plight maiden or else the speeding of my departure."

Then said the King, and his voice was terrible though yet he smiled: "I will not hinder; I will not help. Depart in peace!"

Then Hallblithe turned away dizzy and half fainting, and strayed down the field, scarce knowing where he was; and as he went he felt his sleeve plucked at, and turned about, and lo! he was face to face with the Sea-eagle, no less joyous than aforetime. He took Hallblithe in his arms and embraced him and kissed him, and said: "Well met, faring-fellow! Whither away?"

"Away out of this land of lies," said Hallblithe.

The Sea-eagle shook his head, and quoth he: "Art thou still seeking a dream? And thou so fair that thou puttest all other men to shame."

"I seek no dream," said Hallblithe, "but rather the end of dreams."

"Well," said the Sea-eagle, "we will not wrangle about it. But hearken. Hard by in a pleasant nook of the meadows have I set up my tent; and although it be not as big as the King's pavilion, yet is it fair enough. Wilt thou not come thither with me and rest thee to-night; and to-morrow we will talk of this matter?"

Now Hallblithe was weary and confused, and downhearted beyond his wont, and the friendly words of the Sea-eagle softened his heart, and he smiled on him and said: "I give thee thanks; I will come with thee: thou art kind, and hast done nought to me save good from the time when I first saw thee lying in thy bed in the Hall of the Ravagers. Dost thou remember the day?"

The Sea-eagle knitted his brow as one striving with a troublous memory, and said: "But dimly, friend, as if it had passed in an ugly dream: meseemeth my friendship with thee began when I came to thee from out of the wood, and saw thee standing with those three damsels; that I remember full well ye were fair to look on."

Hallblithe wondered at his words, but said no more about it, and they went together to a flowery nook nigh a stream of clear water where stood a silken tent, green like the grass which it stood on, and flecked with gold and goodly colours. Nigh it on the grass lay the Sea-eagle's damsel, ruddy-cheeked and sweet-lipped, as fair as aforetime. She turned about when she heard men coming, and when she saw Hallblithe a smile came into her face like the sun breaking out on a fair but clouded morning, and she went up to him and took him by the hands and kissed his cheek, and said: "Welcome, Spearman! welcome back! We have heard of thee in many places, and have been sorry that thou wert not glad, and now are we fain of thy returning. Shall not sweet life begin for thee from henceforward?"

Again was Hallblithe moved by her kind welcome; but he shook his head and spake: "Thou art kind, sister; yet if thou wouldst be kinder thou wilt show me a way whereby I may escape from this land. For abiding here has become irksome to me, and meseemeth that hope is yet alive without the Glittering Plain."

Her face fell as she answered: "Yea, and fear also, and worse, if aught be worse. But come, let us eat and drink in this fair place, and gather for thee a little joyance before thou departest, if thou needs must depart."

He smiled on her as one not ill-content, and laid himself down on the grass, while the twain busied themselves, and brought forth fair cushions and a gilded table, and laid dainty victual thereon and good wine.

---

So they ate and drank together, and the Sea-eagle and his mate became very joyous again, and Hallblithe bestirred himself not to be a mar-feast; for he said within himself: "I am departing, and after this time I shall see them no more; and they are kind and blithe with me, and have been aforetime; I will not make their merry hearts sore. For when I am gone I shall be remembered of them but a little while."

# CHAPTER XVI: THOSE THREE GO THEIR WAYS TO THE EDGE OF THE GLITTERING PLAIN

So the evening wore merrily; and they made Hallblithe lie in an ingle of the tent on a fair bed, and he was weary, and slept thereon like a child. But in the morning early they waked him; and while they were breaking their fast they began to speak to him of his departure, and asked him if he had an inkling of the way whereby he should get him gone, and he said: "If I escape it must needs be by way of the mountains that wall the land about till they come down to the sea. For on the sea is no ship and no haven; and well I wot that no man of the land durst or can ferry me over to the land of my kindred, or otherwhere without the Glittering Plain. Tell me therefore (and I ask no more of you), is there any rumour or memory of a way that cleaveth yonder mighty wall of rock to other lands?"

Said the damsel: "There is more than a memory or a rumour: there is a road through the mountains known to all men. For at whiles the earthly pilgrims come into the Glittering Plain thereby; and yet but seldom, so many are the griefs and perils which beset the wayfarers on that road. Whereof thou hadst far better bethink thee in time, and abide here and be happy with us and others who long sore to make thee happy."

"Nay," said Hallblithe, "there is nought to do but tell me of the way, and I will depart at once, blessing you."

Said the Sea-eagle: "More than that at least will we do. May I lose the bliss whereto I have attained, if I go not with thee to the very edge of the land of the Glittering Plain. Shall it not be so, sweetheart?"

"Yea, at least we may do that," said the damsel; and she hung her head as if she were ashamed, and said: "And that is all that thou wilt get from us at most."

Said Hallblithe: "It is enough, and I asked not so much."

Then the damsel busied herself, and set meat and drink in two wallets, and took one herself and gave the other to the Sea-eagle, and said: "We will be thy porters, O Spearman, and will give thee a full wallet from the last house by the Desert of Dread, for when thou hast entered therein, thou mayst well find victual hard to come by: and now let us linger no more since the road is dear to thee."

So they set forth on foot, for in that land men were slow to feel weariness; and turning about the hill of Wood-end, they passed by some broken country, and came at even to a house at the entrance of a long valley, with high and steeply-sloping sides, which seemed, as it were, to cleave the dale country wherein they had fared aforetime. At that house they slept well-guested by its folk, and the next morning took their way down the valley, and the folk of the house stood at the door to watch their departure; for they had told the wayfarers that they had fared but a little way thitherward and knew of no folk who had used that road.

So those three fared down the valley southward all day, ever mounting higher as they went. The way was pleasant and easy, for they went over fair, smooth, grassy lawns betwixt the hill-sides, beside a clear rattling stream that ran northward; at whiles were clumps of tall trees, oak for the most part, and at whiles thickets of thorn and eglantine and other such trees: so that they could rest well shaded when they would.

They passed by no house of men, nor came to any such in the even, but lay down to sleep in a thicket of thorn and eglantine, and rested well, and on the morrow they rose up betimes and went on their ways.

This second day as they went, the hill-sides on either hand grew lower, till at last they died out into a wide plain, beyond which in the southern offing the mountains rose huge and bare. This plain also was grassy and beset with trees and thickets here and there. Hereon they saw wild deer enough, as hart and buck, and roebuck and swine: withal a lion came out of a brake hard by them as they went, and stood gazing on them, so that Hallblithe looked to his weapons, and the Sea-eagle took up a big stone to fight with, being weaponless; but the damsel laughed, and tripped on her way lightly with girt-up gown, and the beast gave no more heed to them.

Easy and smooth was their way over this pleasant wilderness, and clear to see, though but little used, and before nightfall, after they had gone a long way, they came to a house. It was not large nor high, but was built very strongly and fairly of good ashlar: its door was shut, and on the jamb thereof hung a slug-horn. The damsel, who seemed to know what to do, set her mouth to the horn, and blew a blast; and in a little while the door was opened, and a big man clad in red scarlet stood therein: he had no weapons, but was somewhat surly of aspect: he spake not, but stood abiding the word: so the damsel took it up and said: "Art thou not the Warden of the Uttermost House?"

He said: "I am."

Said the damsel: "May we guest here to-night?"

He said: "The house lieth open to you with all that it hath of victual and plenishing: take what ye will, and use what ye will."

They thanked him; but he heeded not their thanks, and withdrew him from them. So they entered and found the table laid in a fair hall of stone carven and painted very goodly; so they ate and drank therein, and Hallblithe was of good heart, and the Sea-eagle and his mate were merry, though they looked softly and shyly on Hallblithe because of the sundering anigh; and they saw no man in the house save the man in scarlet, who went and came about his business, paying no heed to them. So when the night was deep they lay down in the shut-bed off the hall, and slept, and the hours were tidingless to them until they woke in the morning.

On the morrow they arose and broke their fast, and thereafter the damsel spake to the man in scarlet and said: "May we fill our wallets with victual for the way?"

Said the Warden: "There lieth the meat."

So they filled their wallets, while the man looked on; and they came to the door when they were ready, and he unlocked it to them, saying no word. But when they turned their faces towards the mountains he spake at last, and stayed them at the first step. Quoth he: "Whither away? Ye take the wrong road!"

Said Hallblithe: "Nay, for we go toward the mountains and the edge of the Glittering Plain."

"Ye shall do ill to go thither," said the Warden, "and I bid you forbear."

"O Warden of the Uttermost House, wherefore should we forbear?" said the Sea-eagle.

Said the scarlet man: "Because my charge is to further those who would go inward to the King, and to stay those who would go outward from the King."

"How then if we go outward despite thy bidding?" said the Sea-eagle, "wilt thou then hinder us perforce?"

"How may I," said the man, "since thy fellow hath weapons?"

"Go we forth, then," said the Sea-eagle.

"Yea," said the damsel, "we will go forth. And know, O Warden, that this weaponed man only is of mind to fare over the edge of the Glittering Plain; but we twain shall come back hither again, and fare inwards."

Said the Warden: "Nought is it to me what ye will do when you are past this house. Nor shall any man who goeth out of this garth toward the mountains ever come back inwards save he cometh in the company of new-comers to the Glittering Plain."

"Who shall hinder him?" said the Sea-eagle.

"The King," said the Warden.

Then there was silence awhile, and the man said:

"Now do as ye will." And therewith he turned back into the house and shut the door.

But the Sea-eagle and the damsel stood gazing on one another, and at Hallblithe; and the damsel was downcast and pale; but the Sea-eagle cried out:

"Forward now, O Hallblithe, since thou willest it, and we will go with thee and share whatever may befall thee; yea, right up to the very edge of the Glittering Plain. And thou, O beloved, why dost thou delay? Why dost thou stand as if thy fair feet were grown to the grass?"

But the damsel gave a lamentable cry, and cast herself down on the ground, and knelt before the Sea-eagle, and took him by the knees, and said betwixt sobbing and weeping: "O my lord and love, I pray thee to forbear, and the Spearman, our friend, shall pardon us. For if thou goest, I shall never see thee more, since my heart will not serve me to go with thee. O forbear! I pray thee!"

And she grovelled on the earth before him; and the Sea-eagle waxed red, and would have spoken but Hallblithe cut his speech across, and said "Friends, be at peace! For this is the minute that sunders us. Get ye back at once to the heart of the Glittering Plain, and live there and be happy; and take my blessing and thanks for the love and help that ye have given me. For your going forward with me should destroy you and profit me nothing. It would be but as the host bringing his guests one field beyond his garth, when their goal is the ends of the earth; and if there were a lion in the path, why should he perish for courtesy's sake?"

Therewith he stooped down to the damsel, and lifted her up and kissed her face; and he cast his arms about the Sea-eagle and said to him: "Farewell, shipmate!"

---

Then the damsel gave him the wallet of victual, and bade him farewell, weeping sorely; and he looked kindly on them for a moment of time, and then turned away from them and fared on toward the mountains, striding with great strides, holding his head aloft. But they looked no more on him, having no will to eke their sorrow, but went their ways back again without delay.

# CHAPTER XVII: HALLBLITHE AMONGST THE MOUNTAINS

So strode on Hallblithe; but when he had gone but a little way his head turned, and the earth and heavens wavered before him, so that he must needs sit down on a stone by the wayside, wondering what ailed him. Then he looked up at the mountains, which now seemed quite near to him at the plain's ending, and his weakness increased on him; and lo! as he looked, it was to him as if the crags rose up in the sky to meet him and overhang him, and as if the earth heaved up beneath him, and therewith he fell aback and lost all sense, so that he knew not what was become of the earth and the heavens and the passing of the minutes of his life.

When he came to himself he knew not whether he had lain so a great while or a little; he felt feeble, and for a while he lay scarce moving, and beholding nought, not even the sky above him. Presently he turned about and saw hard stone on either side, so he rose wearily and stood upon his feet, and knew that he was faint with hunger and thirst. Then he looked around him, and saw that he was in a narrow valley or cleft of the mountains amidst wan rocks, bare and waterless, where grew no blade of green; but he could see no further than the sides of that cleft, and he longed to be out of it that he might see whitherward to turn. Then he bethought him of his wallet, and set his hand to it and opened it, thinking to get victual thence; but lo! it was all spoilt and wasted. None the less, for all his feebleness, he turned and went toiling slowly along what seemed to be a path little trodden leading upward out of the cleft; and at last he reached the crest thereof, and sat him down on a rock on the other side; yet durst not raise his eyes awhile and look on the land, lest he should see death manifest therein. At last he looked, and saw that he was high up amongst the mountain-peaks: before him and on either hand was but a world of fallow stone rising ridge upon ridge like the waves of the wildest of the winter sea. The sun not far from its midmost shone down bright and hot on that wilderness; yet was there no sign that any man had ever been there since the beginning of the world, save that the path aforesaid seemed to lead onward down the stony slope.

This way and that way and all about he gazed, straining his eyes if perchance he might see any diversity in the stony waste; and at last betwixt two peaks of the rock-wall on his left hand he descried a streak of green mingling with the cold blue of the distance; and he thought in his heart that this was the last he should see of the Glittering Plain. Then he spake aloud in that desert, and said, though there was none to hear: "Now is my last hour come; and here is Hallblithe of the Raven perishing, with his deeds undone and his longing unfulfilled, and his bridal-bed acold for ever. Long may the House of the Raven abide and flourish, with many a man and maiden, valiant and fair and fruitful! O kindred, cast thy blessing on this man about to die here, doing none otherwise than ye would have him!"

He sat there a little while longer, and then he said to himself: "Death tarries; were it not well that I go to meet him, even as the cot-carle preventeth the mighty chieftain?"

Then he arose, and went painfully down the slope, steadying himself with the shaft of his gleaming spear; but all at once he stopped; for it seemed to him that he heard voices borne on the wind that blew up the mountain-side. But he shook his head and said: "Now forsooth beginneth the dream which shall last for ever; nowise am I beguiled by it." None the less he strove the more eagerly with the wind and the way and his feebleness; yet did the weakness wax on him, so that it was but a little while ere he faltered and reeled and fell down once more in a swoon.

When he came to himself again he was no longer alone: a man was kneeling down by him and holding up his head, while another before him, as he opened his eyes, put a cup of wine to his lips. So Hallblithe drank and was refreshed; and presently they gave him bread, and he ate, and his heart was strengthened, and the happiness of life returned to it, and he lay back, and slept sweetly for a season.

When he awoke from that slumber he found that he had gotten back much of his strength again, and he sat up and looked around him, and saw three men sitting anigh, armed and girt with swords, yet in evil array, and sore travel-worn. One of these was very old, with long white hair hanging down; and another, though he was not so much stricken in years, still looked an old man of over sixty winters. The third was a man some forty years old, but sad and sorry and drooping of aspect.

---

So when they saw him stirring, they all fixed their eyes upon him, and the oldest man said: "Welcome to him who erst had no tidings for us!" And the second said: "Tell us now thy tidings." But the third, the sorry man, cried out aloud, saying: "Where is the Land? Where is the Land?"

Said Hallblithe: "Meseemeth the land which ye seek is the land which I seek to flee from. And now I will not hide that meseemeth I have seen you before, and that was at Cleveland by the Sea when the days were happier."

Then they all three bowed their heads in yea-say, and spake: "'Where is the Land? Where is the Land?"

Then Hallblithe arose to his feet, and said: "Ye have healed me of the sickness of death, and I will do what I may to heal you of your sickness of sorrow. Come up the pass with me, and I will show you the land afar off."

Then they arose like young and brisk men, and he led them over the brow of the ridge into the little valley wherein he had first come to himself: there he showed them that glimpse of a green land betwixt the two peaks, which he had beheld e'en now; and they stood a while looking at it and weeping for joy.

Then spake the oldest of the seekers: "Show us the way to the land."

"Nay," said Hallblithe, "I may not; for when I would depart thence, I might not go by mine own will, but was borne out hither, I wot not how. For when I came to the edge of the land against the will of the King, he smote me, and then cast me out. Therefore since I may not help you, find ye the land for yourselves, and let me go blessing you, and come out of this desert by the way whereby ye entered it. For I have an errand in the world."

Spake the youngest of the seekers: "Now art thou become the yoke-fellow of Sorrow, and thou must wend, not whither thou wouldst, but whither she will: and she would have thee go forward toward life, not backward toward death."

Said the midmost seeker: "If we let thee go further into the wilderness thou shalt surely die: for hence to the peopled parts, and the City of Merchants, whence we come, is a month's journey: and there is neither meat nor drink, nor beast nor bird, nor any green thing all that way; and since we have found thee famishing, we may well deem that thou hast no victual. As to us we have but little; so that if it be much more than three days' journey to the Glittering Plain, we may well starve and die within sight of the Acre of the Undying. Nevertheless that little will we share with thee if thou wilt help us to find that good land; so that thou mayst yet put away Sorrow, and take Joy again to thy board and bed."

Hallblithe hung his head and answered nought; for he was confused by the meshes of ill-hap, and his soul grew sick with the bitterness of death. But the sad man spake again and said: "Thou hast an errand sayest thou? is it such as a dead man may do?"

Hallblithe pondered, and amidst the anguish of his despair was borne in on him a vision of the sea-waves lapping the side of a black ship, and a man therein: who but himself, set free to do his errand, and his heart was quickened within him, and he said: "I thank you, and I will wend back with you, since there is no road for me save back again into the trap."

The three seekers seemed glad thereat, and the second one said: "Though death is pursuing, and life lieth ahead, yet will we not hasten thee unduly. Time was when I was Captain of the Host, and learned how battles were lost by lack of rest. Therefore have thy sleep now, that thou mayst wax in strength for our helping."

Said Hallblithe: "I need not rest; I may not rest; I will not rest."

Said the sad man: "It is lawful for thee to rest. So say I, who was once a master of law."

Said the long-hoary elder: "And I command thee to rest; I who was once the king of a mighty folk."

In sooth Hallblithe was now exceeding weary; so he laid him down and slept sweetly in the stony wilderness amidst those three seekers, the old, the sad, and the very old.

When he awoke he felt well and strong again, and he leapt to his feet and looked about him, and saw the three seekers stirring, and he deemed by the sun that it was early morning. The sad man brought forth bread and water and wine, and they broke their fast; and when they had done he spake and said: "Abideth now in wallet and bottle but one more full meal for us, and then no more save a few crumbs and a drop or two of wine if we husband it well."

Said the second elder: "Get we to the road, then, and make haste. I have been seeking, and meseemeth, though the way be long, it is not utterly blind for us. Or look thou, Raven-son, is there not a path yonder that leadeth onward up to the brow of the ghyll again? and as I have seen, it leadeth on again down from the said brow."

Forsooth there was a track that led through the stony tangle of the wilderness; so they took to the road with a good heart, and went all day, and saw no living thing, and not a blade of grass or a trickle of water: nought save the wan rocks under the sun; and though they trusted in their road that it led them aright, they saw no other glimpse of the Glittering Plain, because there rose a great ridge like a wall on the north side, and they went as it were down along a trench of the rocks, albeit it was whiles broken across by ghylls, and knolls, and reefs.

So at sunset they rested and ate their victual, for they were very weary; and thereafter they lay down, and slept as soundly as if they were in the best of the halls of men. On the morrow betimes they arose soberly and went their ways with few words, and, as they deemed, the path still led them onward. And now the great ridge on the north rose steeper and steeper, and their crossing it seemed not to be thought of; but their half-blind track failed them not. They rested at even, and ate and drank what little they had left, save a mouthful or two of wine, and then went on again by the light of the moon, which was so bright that they still saw their way. And it happened to Hallblithe, as mostly it does with men very travel-worn, that he went on and on scarce remembering where he was, or who his fellows were, or that he had any fellows.

So at midnight they lay down in the wilderness again, hungry and weary. They rose at dawn and went forward with waning hope: for now the mountain ridge on the north was close to their path, rising up along a sheer wall of pale stone over which nothing might go save the fowl flying; so that at first on that morning they looked for nothing save to lay their bones in that grievous desert where no man should find them.

But, as beset with famine, they fared on heavily down the narrow track, there came a hoarse cry from Hallblithe's dry throat and it was as if his cry had been answered by another like to his; and the seekers turned and beheld him pointing to the cliff-side, and lo! half-way up the pale sun-litten crag stood two ravens in a cranny of the stone, flapping their wings and croaking, with thrusting forth and twisting of their heads; and presently they came floating on the thin pure air high up over the heads of the wayfarers, croaking for the pleasure of the meeting, as though they laughed thereat.

Then rose the heart of Hallblithe, and he smote his palms together, and fell to singing an old song of his people, amidst the rocks whereas few men had sung aforetime.

Whence are ye and whither, O fowl of our fathers? What field have ye looked on, what acres unshorn?What land have ye left where the battle-folk gathers,And the war-helms are white o'er the paths of the corn?

What tale do ye bear of the people uncraven,Where amidst the long hall-shadow sparkle the spears;Where aloft on the hall-ridge now flappeth the raven,And singeth the song of the nourishing years?

There gather the lads in the first of the morning,While white lies the battle-day's dew on the grass,And the kind steeds trot up to the horn's voice of warning,And the winds wake and whine in the dusk of the pass.

O fowl of our fathers, why now are ye resting?Come over the mountains and look on the foe.Full fair after fight won shall yet be your nesting;And your fledglings the sons of the kindred shall know.

Therewith he strode with his head upraised, and above him flew the ravens, croaking as if they answered his song in friendly fashion.

It was but a little after this that the path turned aside sharp toward the cliffs, and the seekers were abashed thereof, till Hallblithe running forward beheld a great cavern in the face of the cliff at the path's ending: so he turned and cried on his fellows, and they hastened up, and presently stood before that cavern's mouth with doubt and joy mingled in their minds; for now, mayhappen, they had reached the gate of the Glittering Plain, or mayhappen the gate of death.

The sad man hung his head and spake: "Doth not some new trap abide us? What do we here? is this aught save death?"

Spake the Elder of Elders: "Was not death on either hand e'en now, even as treason besetteth the king upon his throne?"

And the second said: "Yea, we were as the host which hath no road save through the multitude of foe-men."

But Hallblithe laughed and said: "Why do ye hang back, then? As for me, if death be here, soon is mine errand sped." Therewith he led the way into the dark of the cave, and the ravens hung about the crag overhead croaking, as the men left the light.

So was their way swallowed up in the cavern, and day and its time became nought to them; they went on and on, and became exceeding faint and weary, but rested not, for death was behind them. Whiles they deemed they heard waters running, and whiles the singing of fowl; and to Hallblithe it seemed that he heard his name called, so that he shouted back in answer; but all was still when the sound of his voice had died out.

At last, when they were pressing on again after a short while of resting, Hallblithe cried out that the cave was lightening: so they hastened onward, and the light grew till they could dimly see each other, and dimly they beheld the cave that it was both wide and high. Yet a little further, and their faces showed white to one another, and they could see the crannies of the rocks, and the bats hanging garlanded from the roof. So then they came to where the day streamed down bright on them from a break overhead, and lo! the sky and green leaves waving against it.

To those way-worn men it seemed hard to clamber out that way, and especially to the elders: so they went on a little further to see if there were aught better abiding them, but when they found the daylight failing them again, they turned back to the place of the break in the roof, lest they should waste their strength and perish in the bowels of the mountain. So with much ado they hove up Hallblithe till he got him first on to a ledge of the rocky wall, and so, what by strength, what by cunning, into the daylight through the rent in the roof. So when he was without he made a rope of his girdle and strips from his raiment, for he was ever a deft craftsman, and made a shift to heave up therewith the sad man, who was light and lithe of body; and then the two together dealt with the elders one after another, till they were all four on the face of the earth again.

The place whereto they had gotten was the side of a huge mountain, stony and steep, but set about with bushes, which seemed full fair to those wanderers amongst the rocks. This mountain-slope went down towards a fair green plain, which Hallblithe made no doubt was the outlying waste of the Glittering Plain: nay, he deemed that he could see afar off thereon the white walls of the Uttermost House. So much he told the seekers in few words; and then while they grovelled on the earth and wept for pure joy, whereas the sun was down and it was beginning to grow dusk, he went and looked around soberly to see if he might find water and any kind of victual; and presently a little down the hillside he came upon a place where a spring came gushing up out of the earth and ran down toward the plain; and about it was green grass growing plentifully, and a little thicket of bramble and wilding fruit-trees. So he drank of the water, and plucked him a few wilding apples somewhat better than crabs, and then went up the hill again and fetched the seekers to that mountain hostelry; and while they drank of the stream he plucked them apples and bramble-berries. For indeed they were as men out of their wits, and were dazed by the extremity of their jog, and as men long shut up in prison, to whom the world of men-folk hath become strange. Simple as the victual was, they were somewhat strengthened by it and by the plentiful water, and as night was now upon them, it was of no avail for them to go further: so they slept beneath the boughs of the thorn-bushes.

# CHAPTER XVIII: HALLBLITHE DWELLETH IN THE WOOD ALONE

But on the morrow they arose betimes, and broke their fast on that woodland victual, and then went speedily down the mountain-side; and Hallblithe saw by the clear morning light that it was indeed the Uttermost House which he had seen across the green waste. So he told the seekers; but they were silent and heeded nought, because of a fear that had come upon them, lest they should die before they came into that good land. At the foot of the mountain they came upon a river, deep but not wide, with low grassy banks, and Hallblithe, who was an exceeding strong swimmer, helped the seekers over without much ado; and there they stood upon the grass of that goodly waste.

Hallblithe looked on them to note if any change should come over them, and he deemed that already they were become stronger and of more avail. But he spake nought thereof, and strode on toward the Uttermost House, even as that other day he had stridden away from it.

Such diligence they made, that it was but little after noon when they came to the door thereof. Then Hallblithe took the horn and blew upon it, while his fellows stood by murmuring, "It is the Land! It is the Land!"

So came the Warden to the door, clad in red scarlet, and the elder went up to him and said: "Is this the Land?"

"What land?" said the Warden.

"Is it the Glittering Plain?" said the second of the seekers.

"Yea, forsooth," said the Warden. Said the sad man: "Will ye lead us to the King?"

"Ye shall come to the King," said the Warden.

"When, oh when?" cried they out all three.

"The morrow of to-morrow, maybe," said the Warden.

"Oh! if to-morrow were but come!" they cried.

"It will come," said the red man; "enter ye the house, and eat and drink and rest you."

So they entered, and the Warden heeded Hallblithe nothing. They ate and drank and then went to their rest, and Hallblithe lay in a shut-bed off from the hall, but the Warden brought the seekers otherwhere, so that Hallblithe saw them not after he had gone to bed; but as for him he slept and forgot that aught was.

In the morning when he awoke he felt very strong and well-liking; and he beheld his limbs that they were clear of skin and sleek and fair; and he heard one hard by in the hall carolling and singing joyously. So he sprang from his bed with the wonder of sleep yet in him, and drew the curtains of the shut-bed and looked forth into the hall; and lo on the high-seat a man of thirty winters by seeming, tall, fair of fashion, with golden hair and eyes as grey as glass, proud and noble of aspect; and anigh him sat another man of like age to look on, a man strong and burly, with short curling brown hair and a red beard, and ruddy countenance, and the mien of a warrior. Also, up and down the hall, paced a man younger of aspect than these two, tall and slender, black-haired and dark-eyed, amorous of countenance; he it was who was singing a snatch of song as he went lightly on the hall pavement: a snatch like to this

Fair is the world, now autumn's wearing,And the sluggard sun lies long abed;Sweet are the days, now winter's nearing,And all winds feign that the wind is dead.

Dumb is the hedge where the crabs hang yellow,Bright as the blossoms of the spring;Dumb is the close where the pears grow mellow,And none but the dauntless redbreasts sing.

Fair was the spring, but amidst his greeningGrey were the days of the hidden sun;Fair was the summer, but overweening,So soon his o'er-sweet days were done.

Come then, love, for peace is upon us,Far off is failing, and far is fear,Here where the rest in the end hath won us,In the garnering tide of the happy year.

Come from the grey old house by the water,Where, far from the lips of the hungry sea,Green groweth the grass o'er the field of the

70

slaughter,And all is a tale for thee and me.

So Hallblithe did on his raiment and went into the hall; and when those three saw him they smiled upon him kindly and greeted him; and the noble man at the board said: "Thanks have thou, O Warrior of the Raven, for thy help in our need: thy reward from us shall not be lacking."

Then the brown-haired man came up to him, and clapped him on the back and said to him: "Brisk man of the Raven, good is thy help at need; even so shall be mine to thee henceforward."

But the young man stepped up to him lightly, and cast his arms about him, and kissed him, and said: "O friend and fellow, who knoweth but I may one day help thee as thou hast holpen me? though thou art one who by seeming mayst well help thyself. And now mayst thou be as merry as I am to-day!"

Then they all three cried out joyously: "It is the Land! It is the Land!"

So Hallblithe knew that these men were the two elders and the sad man of yesterday, and that they had renewed their youth.

Joyously now did those men break their fast: nor did Hallblithe make any grim countenance, for he thought: "That which these dotards and drivellers have been mighty enough to find, shall I not be mighty enough to flee from?" Breakfast done, the seekers made little delay, so eager as they were to behold the King, and to have handsel of their new sweet life. So they got them ready to depart, and the once-captain said: "Art thou able to lead us to the King, O Raven-son, or must we seek another man to do so much for us?"

Said Hallblithe: "I am able to lead you so nigh unto Wood-end (where, as I deem, the King abideth) that ye shall not miss him."

Therewith they went to the door, and the Warden unlocked to them, and spake no word to them when they departed, though they thanked him kindly for the guesting.

When they were without the garth, the young man fell to running about the meadow plucking great handfuls of the rich flowers that grew about, singing and carolling the while. But he who had been king looked up and down and round about, and said at last: "Where be the horses and the men?"

But his fellow with the red beard said: "Raven-son, in this land when they journey, what do they as to riding or going afoot?"

Said Hallblithe: "Fair fellows, ye shall wot that in this land folk go afoot for the most part, both men and women; whereas they weary but

71

little, and are in no haste."

Then the once-captain clapped the once-king on the shoulder, and said: "Hearken, lord, and delay no longer, but gird up thy gown, since here is no mare's son to help thee: for fair is to-day that lies before us, with many a new fair day beyond it."

So Hallblithe led the way inward, thinking of many things, yet but little of his fellows. Albeit they, and the younger man especially, were of many words; for this black-haired man had many questions to ask, chiefly concerning the women, what they were like to look on, and of what mood they were. Hallblithe answered thereto as long as he might, but at last he laughed and said: "Friend, forbear thy questions now; for meseemeth in a few hours thou shalt be as wise hereon as is the God of Love himself."

So they made diligence along the road, and all was tidingless till on the second day at even they came to the first house off the waste. There had they good welcome, and slept. But on the morrow when they arose, Hallblithe spake to the Seekers, and said: "Now are things much changed betwixt us since the time when we first met: for then I had all my desire, as I thought, and ye had but one desire, and well nigh lacked hope of its fulfilment. Whereas now the lack hath left you and come to me. Wherefore even as time agone ye might not abide even one night at the House of the Raven, so hard as your desire lay on you; even so it fareth with me to-day, that I am consumed with my desire, and I may not abide with you; lest that befall which befalleth betwixt the full man and the fasting. Wherefore now I bless you and depart."

They abounded in words of good-will to him, and the once-king said: "Abide with us, and we shall see to it that thou have all the dignities that a man may think of."

And the once-captain said: "Lo, here is mine hand that hath been mighty; never shalt thou lack it for the accomplishment of thine uttermost desire. Abide with us."

Lastly said the young man: "Abide with us, Son of the Raven! Set thine heart on a fair woman, yea even were it the fairest; and I will get her for thee, even were my desire set on her."

But he smiled on them, and shook his head, and said: "All hail to you! but mine errand is yet undone." And therewith he departed.

He skirted Wood-end and came not to it, but got him down to the side of the sea, not far from where he first came aland, but somewhat south of it. A fair oak-wood came down close to the beach of the sea;

it was some four miles end-long and over-thwart. Thither Hallblithe betook him, and in a day or two got him wood-wright's tools from a house of men a little outside the wood, three miles from the sea-shore. Then he set to work and built him a little frame-house on a lawn of the wood beside a clear stream; for he was a very deft wood-wright. Withal he made him a bow and arrows, and shot what he would of the fowl and the deer for his livelihood; and folk from that house and otherwhence came to see him, and brought him bread and wine and spicery and other matters which he needed. And the days wore, and men got used to him, and loved him as if he had been a rare image which had been brought to that land for its adornment; and now they no longer called him the Spearman, but the Wood-lover. And as for him, he took all in patience, abiding what the lapse of days should bring forth.

# CHAPTER XIX: HALLBLITHE BUILDS HIM A SKIFF

After Hallblithe had been housed a little while, and the time was again drawing nigh to the twelfth moon since he had come to the Glittering Plain, he went in the wood one day; and, pondering many things without fixing on any one, he stood before a very great oak-tree and looked at the tall straight bole thereof, and there came into his head the words of an old song which was written round a scroll of the carving over the shut-bed, wherein he was wont to lie when he was at home in the House of the Raven: and thus it said:

I am the oak-tree, and forsoothMen deal by me with little ruth;My boughs they shred, my life they slay,And speed me o'er the watery way.

He looked up into that leafy world for a little and then turned back toward his house; but all day long, whether he were at work or at rest, that posy ran in his head, and he kept on saying it over, aloud or not aloud, till the day was done and he went to sleep.

Then in his sleep he dreamed that an exceeding fair woman stood by his bedside, and at first she seemed to him to be an image of the Hostage. But presently her face changed, and her body and her raiment; and, lo! it was the lovely woman, the King's daughter whom he had seen wasting her heart for the love of him. Then even in his dream shame thereof overtook him, and because of that shame he awoke, and lay awake a little, hearkening the wind going through the woodland boughs, and the singing of the owl who had her dwelling in the hollow oak nigh to his house. Slumber overcame him in a little while, and again the image of the King's daughter came to him in his dream, and again when he looked upon her, shame and pity rose so hotly in his heart that he awoke weeping, and lay a while hearkening to the noises of the night. The third time he slept and dreamed; and once more that image came to him. And now he looked, and saw that she had in her hand a book covered outside with gold and gems, even as he saw it in the orchard-close aforetime: and he beheld her face that it was no longer the face of one sick with sorrow; but glad and clear, and most beauteous.

Now she opened the book and held it before Hallblithe and turned the leaves so that he might see them clearly; and therein were woods and castles painted, and burning mountains, and the wall of the world, and kings upon their thrones, and fair women and warriors, all most lovely to behold, even as he had seen it aforetime in the orchard when he lay lurking amidst the leaves of the bay-tree.

So at last she came to the place in the book wherein was painted Hallblithe's own image over against the image of the Hostage; and he looked thereon and longed. But she turned the leaf, and, lo! on one side the Hostage again, standing in a fair garden of the spring with the lilies all about her feet, and behind her the walls of a house, grey, ancient, and lovely: and on the other leaf over against her was painted a sea rippled by a little wind and a boat thereon sailing swiftly, and one man alone in the boat sitting and steering with a cheerful countenance; and he, who but Hallblithe himself. Hallblithe looked thereon for a while and then the King's daughter shut the book, and the dream flowed into other imaginings of no import.

In the grey dawn Hallblithe awoke, and called to mind his dream, and he leapt from his bed and washed the night from off him in the stream, and clad himself and went the shortest way through the wood to that House of folk aforesaid: and as he went his face was bright and he sang the second part of the carven posy; to wit:

Along the grass I lie forlornThat when a while of time is worn,I may

be filled with war and peaceAnd bridge the sundering of the seas.

He came out of the wood and hastened over the flowery meads of the Glittering Plain, and came to that same house when it was yet very early. At the door he came across a damsel bearing water from the well, and she spake to him and said: "Welcome, Wood-lover! Seldom

74

art thou seen in our garth; and that is a pity of thee. And now I look on thy face I see that gladness hath come into thine heart, and that thou art most fair and lovely. Here then is a token for thee of the increase of gladness." Therewith she set her buckets on the earth, and stood before him, and took him by the ears, and drew down his face to hers and kissed him sweetly. He smiled on her and said: "I thank thee, sister, for the kiss and the greeting; but I come here having a lack."

"Tell us," she said, "that we may do thee a pleasure."

He said: "I would ask the folk to give me timber, both beams and battens and boards; for if I hew in the wood it will take long to season."

"All this is free for thee to take from our wood-store when thou hast broken thy fast with us," said the damsel. "Come thou in and rest thee."

She took him by the hand and they went in together, and she gave him to eat and drink, and went up and down the house, saying to every one: "Here is come the Wood-lover, and he is glad again; come and see him."

So the folk gathered about him, and made much of him. And when they had made an end of breakfast, the head man of the House said to him: "The beasts are in the wain, and the timber abideth thy choosing; come and see."

So he brought Hallblithe to the timber-bower, where he chose for himself all that he needed of oak-timber of the best; and they loaded the wain therewith, and gave him what he would moreover of nails and treenails and other matters; and he thanked them; and they said to him: "Whither now shall we lead thy timber?"

"Down to the sea-side," quoth he, "nighest to my dwelling."

So did they, and more than a score, men and women, went with him, some in the wain, and some afoot. Thus they came down to the sea-shore, and laid the timber on the strand just above high-water mark; and straightway Hallblithe fell to work shaping him a boat, for well he knew the whole craft thereof; and the folk looked on wondering, till the tide had ebbed the little it was wont to ebb, and left the moist sand firm and smooth; then the women left watching Hallblithe's work, and fell to paddling barefoot in the clear water, for there was scarce a ripple on the sea; and the carles came and played with them so that Hallblithe was left alone a while; for this kind of play was new to that folk, since they seldom came down to the sea-side. Thereafter they needs must dance together, and would have had Hallblithe dance with them; and when he naysaid them because he was fain of his work, in all playfulness they fell to taking the adze out of his hand, whereat he became somewhat wroth, and they were afraid and went and had their dance out without him.

By this time the sun was grown very hot, and they came to him again, and lay down about him and watched his work, for they were weary. And one of the women, still panting with the dance, spake as she looked on the loveliness of her limbs, which one of the swains was caressing: "Brother," said she, "great strokes thou smitest; when wilt thou have smitten the last of them, and come to our house again?"

"Not for many days, fair sister," said he, without looking up.

"Alas that thou shouldst talk so," said a carle, rising up from the warm sand; "what shall all thy toil win thee?"

Spake Hallblithe: "Maybe a merry heart, or maybe death."

At that word they all rose up together, and stood huddled together like sheep that have been driven to the croft-gate, and the shepherd hath left them for a little and they know not whither to go. Little by little they got them to the wain and harnessed their beasts thereto, and departed silently by the way that they had come; but in a little time Hallblithe heard their laughter and merry speech across the flowery meadows. He heeded their departure little, but went on working, and worked the sun down, and on till the stars began to twinkle. Then he went home to his house in the wood, and slept and dreamed not, and began again on the morrow with a good heart.

To be short, no day passed that he wrought not his full tale of work, and the days wore, and his ship-wright's work throve. Often the folk of that house, and from otherwhere round about, came down to the strand to watch him working. Nowise did they wilfully hinder him, but whiles when they could get no talk from him, they would speak of him to each other, wondering that he should so toil to sail upon the sea; for they loved the sea but little, and it soon became clear to them that he was looking to nought else: though it may not be said that they deemed he would leave the land for ever. On the other hand, if they hindered him not, neither did they help, saving when he prayed them for somewhat which he needed, which they would then give him blithely.

Of the Sea-eagle and his damsel, Hallblithe saw nought; whereat he was well content, for he deemed it of no avail to make a second sundering of it.

So he worked and kept his heart up, and at last all was ready; he had made him a mast and a sail, and oars, and whatso-other gear there was need of. So then he thrust his skiff into the sea on an evening whenas there were but two carles standing by; for there would often be a score or two of folk. These two smiled on him and bespake him kindly, but would not help him when he bade them set shoulder to her bows and shove. Albeit he got the skiff into the water without much ado, and got into her, and brought her to where a stream running from out of his wood made a little haven for her up from the sea. There he tied her to a tree-hole, and busied himself that even with getting the gear into her, and victual and water withal, as much as he deemed he should need: and so, being weary, he went to his house to sleep, thinking that he should awake in the grey of the morning and thrust out into the deep sea. And he was the more content to abide, because on that eve, as oftenest betid, the wind blew landward from the sea, whereas in the morning it oftenest blew seaward from the land. In any case he thought to be astir so timely that he should come alone to his keel, and depart with no leave-takings. But, as it fell out, he overslept himself, so that when he came out into the wood clad in all his armour, with his sword girt to his side, and his spear over his shoulder, he heard the voices of folk, and presently found so many gathered about his boat that he had some ado to get aboard.

The folk had brought many gifts for him of such things as they deemed he might need for a short voyage, as fruit and wine, and woollen cloths to keep the cold night from him; he thanked them kindly as he stepped over the gunwale, and some of the women kissed him: and one said (she it was, who had met him at the stead that morning when he went to fetch timber): "Thou wilt be back this even, wilt thou not, brother? It is yet but early, and thou shalt have time enough to take all thy pleasure on the sea, and then come back to us to eat thy meat in our house at nightfall."

She spake, knitting her brows in longing for his return; but he knew that all those deemed he would come back again soon; else had they deemed him a rebel of the King, and might, as he thought, have stayed him. So he changed not countenance in any wise, but said only: "farewell, sister, for this day, and farewell to all you till I come back."

Therewith he unmoored his boat, and sat down and took the oars, and rowed till he was out of the little haven, and on the green sea, and the keel rose and fell on the waves. Then he stepped the mast and hoisted sail, and sheeted home, for the morning wind was blowing gently from the mountains over the meadows of the Glittering Plain, so the sail filled, and the keel leapt forward and sped over the face of the cold sea. And it is to be said that whether he wotted or not, it was the very day twelve months since he had come to that shore along with the Sea-eagle. So that folk stood and watched the skiff growing less and less upon the deep till they could scarce see her. Then they turned about and went into the wood to disport them, for the sun was growing hot. Nevertheless, there were some of them (and that damsel was one), who came back to the sea-shore from time to time all day long; and even when the sun was down they looked seaward under the rising moon, expecting to see Hallblithe's bark come into the shining path which she drew across the waters round about the Glittering Land.

# CHAPTER XX: SO NOW SAILETH HALLBLITHE AWAY FROM THE GLITTERING PLAIN

But as to Hallblithe, he soon lost sight of the Glittering Plain and the mountains thereof, and there was nought but sea all round about him, and his heart swelled with joy as he sniffed the brine and watched the gleaming hills and valleys of the restless deep; and he said to himself that he was going home to his Kindred and the Roof of his Fathers of old time.

He stood as near due north as he might; but as the day wore, the wind headed him, and he deemed it not well to beat, lest he should make his voyage overlong; so he ran on with the wind abeam, and his little craft leapt merrily over the sea-hills under the freshening breeze. The sun set and the moon and stars shone out, and he still sailed on, and durst not sleep, save as a dog does, with one eye. At last came dawn, and as the light grew it was a fair day with a falling wind, and a bright sky, but it clouded over before sunset, and the wind freshened from the north by east, and, would he, would he not, Hallblithe must run before it night-long, till at sunrise it fell again, and all day was too light for him to make much way beating to northward; nor did it freshen till after the moon was risen some while after sunset. And now he was so weary that he must needs sleep; so he lashed the helm, and took a reef in the sail, and ran before the wind, he sleeping in the stern.

But past the middle of the night, towards the dawning, he awoke with the sound of a great shout in his ears. So he looked over the dark waters, and saw nought, for the night was cloudy again. Then he trimmed his craft, and went to sleep again, for he was over-burdened with slumber.

When he awoke it was broad daylight; so he looked to the tiller and got the boat's head a little up to the wind, and then gazed about him with the sleep still in his eyes. And as his eyes took in the picture before him he could not refrain a cry; for lo! there arose up great and grim right ahead the black cliffs of the Isle of Ransom. Straightway he got to the sheet, and strove to wear the boat; but for all that he could do she drifted toward the land, for she was gotten into a strong current of the sea that set shoreward. So he struck sail, and took the oars and rowed mightily so that he might bear her off shore; but it availed nothing, and still he drifted landward. So he stood up from the oars, and turned about and looked, and saw that he was but some three furlongs from the shore, and that he was come to the very haven-mouth whence he had set sail with the Sea-eagle a twelvemonth ago: and he knew that into that haven he needs must get him, or be dashed to pieces against the high cliffs of the land: and he saw how the waves ran on to the cliffs, and whiles one higher than the others smote the rock-wall and ran up it, as if it could climb over on to the grassy lip beyond, and then fell back again, leaving a river of brine running down the steep.

Then he said that he would take what might befall him inside the haven. So he hoisted sail again, and took the tiller, and steered right for the midmost of the gate between the rocks, wondering what should await him there. Then it was but a few minutes ere his bark shot into the smoothness of the haven, and presently began to lose way; for all the wind was dead within that land-locked water. Hallblithe looked steadily round about seeking his foe; but the haven was empty of ship or boat; so he ran his eye along the shore to see where he should best lay his keel and as aforesaid there was no beach there, and the water was deep right up to the grassy lip of the land; though the tides ran somewhat high, and at low water would a little steep undercliff go up from the face of the sea. But now it was near the top of the tide, and there was scarce two feet betwixt the grass and the dark-green sea.

Now Hallblithe steered toward an ingle of the haven; and beyond it, a little way off, rose a reef of rocks out of the green grass, and thereby was a flock of sheep feeding, and a big man lying down amongst them, who seemed to be unarmed, as Hallblithe could not see any glint of steel about him. Hallblithe drew nigh the shore, and the big man stirred not; nor did he any the more when the keel ran along the shore, and Hallblithe leapt out and moored his craft to his spear stuck deep in the earth. And now Hallblithe deems that the man must be either dead or asleep: so he drew his sword and had it in his right hand, and in his left a sharp knife, and went straight up to the man betwixt the

---

79

sheep, and found him so lying on his side that he could not see his face; so he stirred him with his foot, and cried out: "Awake, O Shepherd! for dawn is long past and day is come, and therewithal a guest for thee!"

The man turned over and slowly sat up, and, lo! who should it be but the Puny Fox? Hallblithe started back at the sight of him, and cried out at him, and said: "Have I found thee, O mine enemy?"

The Puny Fox sat up a little straighter, and rubbed his eyes and said: "Yea, thou hast found me sure enough. But as to my being thine enemy, a word or two may be said about that presently."

"What!" said Hallblithe, "dost thou deem that aught save my sword will speak to thee?"

"I wot not," said the Puny Fox, slowly rising to his feet, "but I suppose thou wilt not slay me unarmed, and thou seest that I have no weapons."

"Get thee weapons, then," quoth Hallblithe, "and delay not; for the sight of thee alive sickens me."

"Ill is that," said the Puny Fox, "but come thou with me at once, where I shall find both the weapons and a good fighting-stead. Hasten! time presseth, now thou art come at last."

"And my boat?" said Hallblithe.

"Wilt thou carry her in thy pouch?" said the Puny Fox; "thou wilt not need her again, whether thou slay me, or I thee."

Hallblithe knit his brows on him in his wrath; for he deemed that Fox's meaning was to threaten him with the vengeance of the kindred. Howbeit, he said nought; for he deemed it ill to wrangle in words with one whom he was presently to meet in battle; so he followed as the Puny Fox led. Fox brought him past the reef of rock aforesaid, and up a narrow cleft of the cliffs overlooking the sea, whereby they came into a little grass-grown meadow well nigh round in shape, as smooth and level as a hall-floor, and fenced about by a wall of rock: a place which had once been the mouth of an earth-fire, and a cauldron of molten stone.

When they stood on the smooth grass Fox said: "Hold thee there a little, while I go to my weapon-chest, and then shall we see what is to be done."

Therewith he turned aside to a cranny of the rock, and going down on his hands and knees, fell to creeping like a worm up a hole therein, which belike led to a cavern; for after his voice had come forth from the earth, grunting and groaning, and cursing this thing, and that, out he comes again feet first, and casts down an old rusty sword without a sheath; a helm no less rusty, and battered withal, and a round target, curled up and outworn as if it would fall to pieces of itself. Then he stands up and stretches himself, and smiles pleasantly on Hallblithe and says: "Now, mine enemy, when I have donned helm and shield and got my sword in hand, we may begin the play: as to a hauberk I must needs go lack; for I could not come by it; I think the old man must have chaffered it away: he was ever too money-fain."

But Hallblithe looked on him angrily and said: "Hast thou brought me hither to mock me? Hast thou no better weapons wherewith to meet a warrior of the Raven than these rusty shards, which look as if thou hadst robbed a grave of the dead? I will not fight thee so armed."

"Well," said the Puny Fox, "and from out of a grave come they verily: for in that little hole lieth my father's grandsire, the great Sea-mew of the Ravagers, the father of that Sea-eagle whom thou knowest. But since thou thinkest scorn of these weapons of a dead warrior, in go the old carle's treasures again! It is as well maybe; since he might be wrath beyond his wont if he were to wake and miss them; and already this cold cup of the once-boiling rock is not wholly safe because of him."

So he crept into the hole once more, and out of it presently, and stood smiting his palms one against the other to dust them, like a man who has been handling parchments long laid by; and Hallblithe stood looking at him, still wrathful, but silent.

Then said the Puny Fox: "This at least was a wise word of thine, that thou wouldst not fight me. For the end of fighting is slaying; and it is stark folly to fight without slaying; and now I see that thou desirest not to slay me: for if thou didst, why didst thou refuse to fall on me armed with the ghosts of weapons that I borrowed from a ghost? Nay, why didst thou not slay me as I crept out of yonder hole? Thou wouldst have had a cheap bargain of me either way. It would be rank folly to fight me."

Said Hallblithe hoarsely: "Why didst thou bewray me, and lie to me, and lure me away from the quest of my beloved, and waste a whole year of my life?"

"It is a long story," said the Puny Fox, "which I may tell thee some day. Meantime I may tell thee this, that I was compelled thereto by one far mightier than I, to wit the Undying King."

At that word the smouldering wrath blazed up in Hallblithe, and he drew his sword hastily and hewed at the Puny Fox: but he leapt aside nimbly and ran in on Hallblithe, and caught his sword-arm by the

---

81

wrist, and tore the weapon out of his hand, and overbore him by sheer weight and stature, and drave him to the earth. Then he rose up, and let Hallblithe rise also, and took his sword and gave it into his hand again and said: "Crag-nester, thou art wrathful, but little. Now thou hast thy sword again and mayst slay me if thou wilt. Yet not until I have spoken a word to thee: so hearken! or else by the Treasure of the Sea I will slay thee with my bare hands. For I am strong indeed in this place with my old kinsman beside me. Wilt thou hearken?"

"Speak," said Hallblithe, "I hearken."

Said the Puny Fox: "True it is that I lured thee away from thy quest, and wore away a year of thy life. Yet true it is also that I repent me thereof, and ask thy pardon. What sayest thou?"

Hallblithe spake not, but the heat died out of his face and he was become somewhat pale. Said the Puny Fox: "Dost thou not remember, O Raven, how thou badest me battle last year on the sea-shore by the side of the Rollers of the Raven? and how this was to be the prize of battle, that the vanquished should serve the vanquisher year-long, and do all his will? And now this prize and more thou hast won without battle; for I swear by the Treasure of the Sea, and by the bones of the great Sea-mew yonder, that I will serve thee not year-long but life-long, and that I will help thee in thy quest for thy beloved. What sayest thou?"

Hallblithe stood speechless a moment, looking past the Puny Fox, rather than at him. Then the sword tumbled out of his hand on to the grass, and great tears rolled down his cheeks and fell on to his raiment, and he reached out his hand to the Puny Fox and said: "O friend, wilt thou not bring me to her? for the days wear, and the trees are growing old round about the Acres of the Raven."

Then the Puny Fox took his hand; and laughed merrily in his face, and said: "Great is thine heart, O Carrion-biter! But now that thou art my friend I will tell thee that I have a deeming of the whereabouts of thy beloved. Or where deemest thou was the garden wherein thou sawest her standing on the page of the book in that dream of the night? So it is, O Raven-son, that it is not for nothing that my grandsire's father lieth in yonder hole of the rocks; for of late he hath made me wise in mighty lore. Thanks have thou, O kinsman!" And he turned him toward the rock wherein was the grave.

But Hallblithe said: "What is to do now? Am I not in a land of foemen?"

"Yea, forsooth," said the Puny Fox, "and even if thou knewest where thy love is, thou shouldst hardly escape from this isle unslain, save for me."

Said Hallblithe: "Is there not my bark, that I might depart at once? for I deem not that the Hostage is on the Isle of Ransom."

The Puny Fox laughed boisterously and said: "Nay, she is not. But as to thy boat, there is so strong a set of the flood-tide toward this end of the isle, that with the wind blowing as now, from the north-north-east, thou mayst not get off the shore for four hours at least, and I misdoubt me that within that time we shall have tidings of a ship of ours coming into the haven. Thy bark they shall take, and thee also if thou art therein; and then soon were the story told, for they know thee for a rebel of the Undying King. Hearken! Dost thou not hear the horn's voice? Come up hither and we shall see what is towards."

So saying, he led hastily up a kind of stair in the rock-wall, until they reached a cranny, whence through a hole in the cliff, they could see all over the haven. And lo! as they looked, in the very gate and entry of it came a great ship heaving up her bows on the last swell of the outer sea (where the wind had risen somewhat), and rolling into the smooth, land-locked water. Black was her sail, and the image of the Sea-eagle enwrought thereon spread wide over it; and the banner of the Flaming Sword streamed out from the stern. Many men all-weaponed were on the decks, and the minstrels high up on the poop were blowing a merry song of return on their battle-horns.

"Lo, you," said the Puny Fox, "thy luck or mine hath served thee this time, in that the Flaming Sword did not overhaul thee ere thou madest the haven. We are well here at least."

Said Hallblithe: "But may not some of them come up hither perchance?"

"Nay, nay," said the Puny Fox; "they fear the old man in the cleft yonder; for he is not over guest-fain. This mead is mine own, as for other living men; it is my unroofed house, and I have here a house with a roof also, which I will show thee presently. For now since the Flaming Sword hath come, there is no need for haste; nay, we cannot depart till they have gone up-country. So I will show thee presently what we shall do to-night."

So there they sat and watched those men bring their ship to the shore and moor her hard by Hallblithe's boat. They cried out when they saw her, and when they were aland they gathered about her to note her build, and the fashion of the spear whereto she was tied. Then in a while the more part of them, some fourscore in number, departed up the valley toward the great house and left none but a half dozen ship-warders behind.

"Seest thou, friend of the Ravens," said the Fox, "hadst thou been there, they might have done with thee what they would. Did I not well to bring thee into my unroofed house?"

"Yea, verily," said Hallblithe; "but will not some of the ship-wards, or some of the others returning, come up hither and find us? I shall yet lay my bones in this evil island."

The Puny Fox laughed, and said: "It is not so bad as thy sour looks would have it; anyhow it is good enough for a grave, and at this present I may call it a casket of precious things."

"What meanest thou?" said Hallblithe eagerly.

"Nay, nay," said the other, "nought but what thou knowest. Art thou not therein, and I myself? without reckoning the old carle in the hole yonder. But I promise thee thou shalt not die here this time, unless thou wilt. And as to folk coming up hither, I tell thee again they durst not; because they fear my great-grandsire over much. Not that they are far wrong therein; for now he is dead, the worst of him seemeth to come out of him, and he is not easily dealt with, save by one who hath some share of his wisdom. Thou thyself couldst see by my kinsman, the Sea-eagle, how much of ill blood and churlish malice there may be in our kindred when they wax old, and loneliness and dreariness taketh hold of them. For I must tell thee that I have oft heard my father say that his father the Sea-eagle was in his youth and his prime blithe and buxom, a great lover of women, and a very friendly fellow. But ever, as I say, as the men of our kind wax in years, they worsen; and thereby mayst thou deem how bad the old man in yonder must be, since he hath lain so long in the grave. But now we will go to that house of mine on the other side of the mead, over against my kinsman's."

Therewith he led Hallblithe down from the rock while Hallblithe said to him: "What! art thou also dead that thou hast a grave here?"

"Nay, nay," said Fox, smiling, "am I so evil-conditioned then? I am no older than thou art."

"But tell me," said Hallblithe, "wilt thou also wax evil as thou growest old?"

"Maybe not," said Fox, looking hard at him, "for in my mind it is that I may be taken into another house, and another kindred, and amongst them I shall be healed of much that might turn to ill."

Therewith were they come across the little meadow to a place

---

84

where was a cave in the rock closed with a door, and a wicket window therein. Fox led Hallblithe into it, and within it was no ill dwelling; for it was dry and clean, and there were stools therein and a table, and shelves and lockers in the wall. When they had sat them down Fox said: "Here mightest thou dwell safely as long as thou wouldst, if thou wouldst risk dealings with the old carle. But, as I wot well that thou art in haste to be gone and get home to thy kindred, I must bring thee at dusk to-day close up to our feast-hall, so that thou mayst be at hand to do what hath to be done to-night, so that we may get us gone to-morrow. Also thou must do off thy Raven gear lest we meet any in the twilight as we go up to the house; and here have I to hand home-spun raiment such as our war-taken thralls wear, which shall serve thy turn well enough; but this thou needst not do on till the time is at hand for our departure; and then I will bring thee away, and bestow thee in a bower hard by the hall; and when thou art within, I may so look to it that none shall go in there, or if they do, they shall see nought in thee save a carle known to them by name. My kinsman hath learned me to do harder things than this. But now it is time to eat and drink."

Therewith he drew victual from out a locker and they fell to. But when they had eaten, Fox taught Hallblithe what he should do in the hall that night, as shall be told hereafter. And then, with much talk about many things, they wore away the day in that ancient cup of the seething rock, and a little before dusk set out for the hall, bearing with them Hallblithe's gear bundled up together, as though it had been wares from over sea. So they came to the house before the tables were set, and the Puny Fox bestowed Hallblithe in a bower which gave into the buttery, so that it was easy to go straight into the mid-most of the hall. There was Hallblithe clad and armed in his Raven gear; but Fox gave him a vizard to go over his face, so that none might know him when he entered therein.

# CHAPTER XXI: OF THE FIGHT OF THE CHAMPIONS IN THE HALL OF THE RAVAGERS

Now it is to be told that the chieftains came into the hall that night and sat down at the board on the dais, even as Hallblithe had seen them do aforetime. And the chieftain of all, who was called the Erne of the Sea-eagles, rose up according to custom and said: "Hearken, folk! this is a night of the champions, whereon we may not eat till the pale blades have clashed together, and one hath vanquished and another been overcome. Now let them stand forth and give out the prize of victory which the vanquished shall pay to the vanquisher. And let it be known, that, whosoever may be the champion that winneth the battle, whether he be a kinsman, or an alien, or a foeman declared; yea, though he have left the head of my brother at the hall-door, he shall pass this night with us safe from sword, safe from axe, safe from hand: he shall eat as we eat, drink as we drink, sleep as we sleep, and depart safe from any hand or weapon, and shall sail the sea at his pleasure in his own keel or in ours, as to him and us may be meet. Blow up horns for the champions!"

So the horns blew a cheerful strain, and when they were done, there came into the hall a tall man clad in black, and with black armour and weapons saving the white blade of his sword. He had a vizard over his face, but his hair came down from under his helm like the tail of a red horse.

So he stood amidst the floor and cried out: "I am the champion of the Ravagers. But I swear by the Treasure of the Sea that I will cross no blade to-night save with an alien, a foeman of the kindred. Hearest thou, O chieftain, O Erne of the Sea-eagles?"

"Hear it I do," said the chieftain, "and I deem that thy meaning is that we should go supperless to bed; and this cometh of thy perversity: for we know thee despite thy vizard. Belike thou deemest that thou shalt not be met this even, and that there is no free alien in the island to draw sword against thee. But beware! For when we came aland this morning we found a skiff of the aliens tied to a great spear stuck in the bank of the haven; so that there will be one foeman at least abroad in the island. But we said if we should come on the man, we would set his head on the gable of the hall with the mouth open toward the North for a token of reproach to the dwellers in the land over sea. But now give out the prize of victory, and I swear by the Treasure of the Sea that we will abide by thy word."

Said the champion: "These are the terms and conditions of the battle; that whichso of us is vanquished, he shall either die, or serve the vanquisher for twelve moons, to fare with him at his will, to go his errands, and do according to his commandment in all wise. Hearest thou, chieftain?"

"Yea," said he, "and by the Undying King, both thou and we shall abide by this bargain. So look to it that thou smite great strokes, lest our hall lack a gable-knop. Horns, blow up for the alien champion!"

So again the horns were winded; and ere their voice had died, in from the buttery screens came a glittering image of war, and there stood the alien champion over against the warrior of the sea; and he too had a vizard over his face.

Now when the folk saw him, and how slim and light and small he looked beside their champion, and they beheld the Raven painted on his white shield, they hooted and laughed for scorn of him and his littleness. But he tossed his sword up lightly and caught it by the hilts as it fell, and drew nigher to the champion of the sea and stood facing him within reach of his sword. Then the chieftain on the high-seat put his two hands to his mouth and roared out: "Fall on, ye champions, fall on!"

But the folk in the hall were so eager that they stood on the benches and the boards, and craned over each other's shoulders, so that they might lose no whit of the hand-play. Now flashed the blades in the candle-lit hall, and the red-haired champion hove up his sword and smote two great strokes to right and to left; but the alien gave way before him, and the folk cried out at him in scorn and in joy of their champion, who fell to raining down great strokes like the hail amidst the lightning. But so deft was the alien, that he stood amidst it unhurt, and laid many strokes on his foeman, and did all so lightly and easily, that it seemed as if he were dancing rather than fighting; and the folk held their peace and began to doubt if their huge champion would prevail. Now the red-haired fetched a mighty stroke at the alien, who leapt aside lightly and gat his sword in his left hand and dealt a great stroke on the other's head, and the red-haired staggered, for he had over-reached himself; and again the alien smote him a left-handed stroke so that he fell full length on the floor with a mighty clatter, and the sword flew out of his hand: and the folk were dumb-founded.

Then the alien threw himself on the sea-champion, and knelt upon him, and shortened his sword as if to slay him with a thrust. But thereon the man overthrown cried out: "Hold thine hand, for I am vanquished! Now give me peace according to the bargain struck between us, that I shall serve thee year-long, and follow thee wheresoever thou goest."

Therewith the alien champion arose and stood off from him, and the man of the sea gat to his feet, and did off his helm, so that all men could see that he was the Puny Fox.

Then the victorious champion unhelmed himself, and lo, it was Hallblithe! And a shout arose in the hall, part of wonder, part of wrath.

---

Then cried out the Puny Fox: "I call on all men here to bear witness that by reason of this battle, Hallblithe of the Ravens is free to come and go as he will in the Isle of Ransom, and to take help of any man that will help him, and to depart from the isle when he will and how he will, taking me with him if so he will."

Said the chieftain: "Yea, this is right and due, and so shall it be. But now, since no freeman, who is not a foe of the passing hour, may abide in our hall without eating of our meat, come up here, Hallblithe, and sit by me, and eat and drink of the best we have, since the Norns would not give us thine head for a gable-knop. But what wilt thou do with thy thrall the Puny Fox; and whereto in the hall wilt thou have him shown? Or wilt thou that he sit fasting in the darkness to-night, laid in gyves and fetters? Or shall he have the cheer of whipping and stripes, as befitteth a thrall to whom the master oweth a grudge? What is thy will with him?"

Said Hallblithe: "My will is that thou give him a seat next to me, whether that be high or low, or the bench of thy prison-house. That he eat of my dish, and drink of my cup, whatsoever the meat and drink may be. For to-morrow I mean that we twain shall go under the earth-collar together, and that our blood shall run together and that we shall be brothers in arms henceforward." Then Hallblithe did on his helm again and drew his sword, and looked aside to the Puny Fox to bid him do the like, and he did so, and Hallblithe said: "Chieftain, thou hast bidden me to table, and I thank thee; but I will not set my teeth in meat, out of our own house and land, which hath not been truly given to me by one who wotteth of me, unless I have conquered it as a prey of battle; neither will I cast a lie into the loving-cup which shall pass from thy lips to mine: therefore I will tell thee, that though I laid a stroke or two on the Puny Fox, and those no light ones, yet was this battle nought true and real, but a mere beguiling, even as that which I saw foughten in this hall aforetime, when meseemeth the slain men rose up in time to drink the good-night cup. Therefore, O men of the Ravagers, and thou, O Puny Fox, there is nought to bind your hands and refrain your hearts, and ye may slay me if ye will without murder or dishonour, and may make the head of Hallblithe a knop for your feast-hall. Yet shall one or two fall to earth before I fall."

Therewith he shook his sword aloft, and a great roar arose, and weapons came down from the wall, and the candles shone on naked steel. But the Puny Fox came and stood by Hallblithe, and spake in his ear amidst the uproar: "Well now, brother-in-arms, I have been trying to learn thee the lore of lies, and surely thou art the worst scholar who was ever smitten by master. And the outcome of it is that I, who have lied so long and well, must now pay for all, and die for a barren truth."

Said Hallblithe: "Let all be as it will! I love thee, lies and all; but as for me I cannot handle them. Lo you! great and grim shall be the slaying, and we shall not fall unavenged."

Said the Puny Fox: "Hearken! for still they hang back. Belike it is I that have drawn this death on thee and me. My last lie was a fool's lie and we die for it: for what wouldst thou have done hadst thou wotted that thy beloved, the Hostage of the Rose—" He broke off perforce; for Hallblithe was looking to right and left and handling his sword, and heard not that last word of his; and from both sides of the hall the throng was drawing round about those twain, weapon in hand. Then Hallblithe set his eyes on a big man in front who was heaving up a heavy short-sword and thought that he would at least slay this one. But or ever he might smite, the great horn blared out over the tumult, and men forbore a while and fell somewhat silent.

Then came down to them the voice of the chieftain, a loud voice, but clear and with mirth mingled with anger in it, and he said: "What do these fools of the Ravagers cumbering the floor of the feast-hall, and shaking weapons when there is no foeman anigh? Are they dreaming-drunk before the wine is poured? Why do they not sit down in their places, and abide the bringing in of the meat? And ye women, where are ye, why do ye delay our meat, when ye may well wot that our hearts are drooping for hunger; and all hath been duly done, the battle of the champions fought and won, and the prize of war given forth and taken? How long, O folk, shall your chieftains sit fasting?"

Then there arose great laughter in the hall, and men withdrew them from those twain and went and sat them down in their places.

Then the chieftain said: "Come up hither, I say, O Hallblithe, and bring thy war-thrall with thee if thou wilt. But delay not, unless it be so that thou art neither hungry nor thirsty; and good sooth thou shouldst be both; for men say that the ravens are hard to satisfy. Come then and make good cheer with us!"

So Hallblithe thrust his sword into the sheath, and the Puny Fox did the like, and they went both together up the hall to the high-seat. And Hallblithe sat down on the chieftain's right hand, and the Puny Fox next to him; and the chieftain, the Erne, said: "O Hallblithe, dost thou need thine armour at table; or dost thou find it handy to take thy meat clad in thy byrny and girt with a sword?"

Then laughed Hallblithe and said: "Nay, meseemeth to-night I shall need war-gear no more." And he stood up and did off all his armour and gave it, sword and all, into the hands of a woman, who bore it off, he knew not whither. And the Erne looked on him and said: "Well is that! and now I see that thou art a fair young man, and it is no marvel though maidens desire thee."

As he spake came in the damsels with the victual and the cheer was exceeding good, and Hallblithe grew light-hearted.

But when the healths had been drunk as aforetime, and men had drunk a cup or two thereafter, there rose a warrior from one of the endlong benches, a big young man, black-haired and black-bearded, ruddy of visage, and he said in a voice that was rough and fat: "O Erne, and ye other chieftains, we have been talking here at our table concerning this guest of thine who hath beguiled us, and we are not wholly at one with thee as to thy dealings with him. True it is, now that the man hath our meat in his belly, that he must depart from amongst us with a whole skin, unless of his own will he stand up to fight some man of us here. Yet some of us think that he is not so much our friend that we should help him to a keel whereon to fare home to those that hate us: and we say that it would not be unlawful to let the man abide in the isle, and proclaim him a wolf's-head within a half-moon of to-day. Or what sayest thou?"

Said the Erne: "Wait for my word a while, and hearken to another! Is the Grey-goose of the Ravagers in the hall? Let him give out his word on this matter."

Then arose a white-headed carle from a table nigh to the dais, whose black raiment was well adorned with gold. Despite his years his face was fair and little wrinkled; a man with a straight nose and a well-fashioned mouth, and with eyes still bright and grey. He spake: "O folk, I find that the Erne hath done well in cherishing this guest. For first, if he hath beguiled us, he did it not save by the furtherance and sleight of our own kinsman; therefore if any one is to die for beguiling us, let it be the Puny Fox. Secondly, we may well wot that heavy need hath driven the man to this beguilement; and I say that it was no unmanly deed for him to enter our hall and beguile us with his sleight; and that he hath played out the play right well and cunningly with the wisdom of a warrior. Thirdly, the manliness of him is well proven, in that having overcome us in sleight, he hath spoken out the sooth concerning our beguilement and hath made himself our foeman and captive, when he might have sat down by us as our guest, freely and in

---

all honour. And this he did, not as contemning the Puny Fox and his lies and crafty wiles (for he hath told us that he loveth him); but so that he might show himself a man in that which trieth manhood. Moreover, ye shall not forget that he is the rebel of the Undying King, who is our lord and master; therefore in cherishing him we show ourselves great-hearted, in that we fear not the wrath of our master. Therefore I naysay the word of the War-brand that we should make this man a wolf's-head; for in so doing we shall show ourselves lesser-hearted than he is, and of no account beside of him; and his head on our hall-gable should be to us a nithing-stake, and a tree of reproach. So I bid thee, O Erne, to make much of this man; and thou shalt do well to give him worthy gifts, such as warriors may take, so that he may show them at home in the House of the Raven, that it may be the beginning of peace betwixt us and his noble kindred. This is my say, and later on I shall wax no wiser."

Therewith he sat down, and there arose a murmur and stir in the hall; but the more part said that the Grey-goose had spoken well, and that it was good to be at peace with such manly fellows as the new guest was.

But the Erne said: "One word will I lay hereto, to wit, that he who desireth mine enmity let him do scathe to Hallblithe of the Ravens and hinder him."

Then he bade fill round the cups, and called a health to Hallblithe, and all men drank to him, and there was much joyance and merriment.

But when the night was well worn, the Erne turned to Hallblithe and said: "That was a good word of the Grey-goose which he spake concerning the giving of gifts: Raven-son, wilt thou take a gift of me and be my friend?"

"Thy friend will I be," said Hallblithe, "but no gift will I take of thee or any other till I have the gift of gifts, and that is my troth-plight maiden. I will not be glad till I can be glad with her."

Then laughed the Erne, and the Puny Fox grinned all across his wide face, and Hallblithe looked from one to the other of them and wondered at their mirth, and when they saw his wondering eyes, they did but laugh the more; and the Erne said: "Nevertheless, thou shalt see the gift which I would give thee; and then mayst thou take it or leave it as thou wilt. Ho ye! bring in the throne of the Eastland with them that minister to it!"

Certain men left the hall as he spake, and came back bearing with them a throne fashioned most goodly of ivory, parcel-gilt and begemmed, and adorned with marvellous craftsmanship: and they set it down amidst of the hall-floor and went aback to their places, while the Erne sat and smiled kindly on the folk and on Hallblithe. Then arose the sound of fiddles and the lesser harp, and the doors of the screen were opened, and there flowed into the hall a company of fair damsels not less than a score, each one with a rose on her bosom, and they came and stood in order behind the throne of the Eastlands, and they strewed roses on the ground before them: and when they were duly ranged they fell to singing:

Now waneth spring,     While all birds sing,     And the south wind blows     The earliest rose     To and fro     By the doors we know,     And the scented gale     Fills every dale.Slow now are brooks running because of the weed,And the thrush hath no cunning to hide her at need,So swift as she flieth from hedge-row to treeAs one that toil trieth, and deedful must be.

And O! that at last,     All sorrows past,     This night I lay 'Neath the oak-beams grey!     O, to wake from sleep,     To see dawn creep     Through the fruitful grove     Of the house that I love!O! my feet to be treading the threshold once more,O'er which once went the leading of swords to the war!O! my feet in the garden's edge under the sun,Where the seeding grass hardens for haysel begun!

Lo, lo! the wind blows     To the heart of the Rose,     And the ship lies tied     To the haven side!     But O for the keel     The sails to feel!     And the alien ness     Growing less and less;As down the wind driveth and thrusts through the seaThe sail-burg that striveth to turn and go free,But the lads at the tiller they hold her in hand,And the wind our well-willer drives fierce to the land.

We shall wend it yet,     The highway wet;     For what is this     That our bosoms kiss?     What lieth sweet     Before our feet?     What token hath come     To lead us home?'Tis the Rose of the garden walled round from the croftWhere the grey roof its warden steep riseth aloft,'Tis the Rose 'neath the oaken-beamed hall, where they bide,The pledges unbroken, the hand of the bride.

Hallblithe heard the song, and half thought it promised him somewhat; but then he had been so misled and mocked at, that he scarce knew how to rejoice at it.

Now the Erne spake: "Wilt thou not take the chair and these dainty song-birds that stand about it? Much wealth might come into thine hall if thou wert to carry them over sea to rich men who have no kindred, nor affinity wherein to wed, but who love women as well as other men."

Said Hallblithe: "I have wealth enow were I once home again. As to these maidens, I know by the fashion of them that they are no women of the Rose, as by their song they should be. Yet will I take any of these maidens that have will to go with me and be made sisters of my sisters, and wed with the warriors of the Rose; or if they are of a kindred, and long to sit each in the house of her folk, then will we send them home over the sea with warriors to guard them from all trouble. For this gift I thank thee. As to thy throne, I bid thee keep it till a keel cometh thy way from our land, bringing fair gifts for thee and thine. For we are not so unwealthy."

Those that sat nearby heard his words and praised them; but the Erne said: "All this is free to thee, and thou mayst do what thou wilt with the gifts given to thee. Yet shalt thou have the throne; and I have thought of a way to make thee take it. Or what sayst thou, Puny Fox?"

Said the Puny Fox: "Yea if thou wilt, thou mayst, but I thought it not of thee that thou wouldst. Now is all well."

Again Hallblithe looked from one to the other and wondered what they meant. But the Erne cried out: "Bring in now the sitter, who shall fill the empty throne!"

Then again the screen-doors opened, and there came in two weaponed men, leading between them a woman clad in gold and garlanded with roses. So fair was the fashion of her face and all her body, that her coming seemed to make a change in the hall, as though the sun had shone into it suddenly. She trod the hall-floor with firm feet, and sat down on the ivory chair. But even before she was seated therein Hallblithe knew that the Hostage was under that roof and coming toward him. And the heart rose in his breast and fluttered therein, so sore he yearned toward the Daughter of the Rose, and his very speech-friend. Then he heard the Erne saying, "How now, Raven-son, wilt thou have the throne and the sitter therein, or wilt thou gainsay me once more?"

Thereafter he himself spake, and the sound of his voice was strange to him and as if he knew it not: "Chieftain, I will not gainsay thee, but will take thy gift, and thy friendship therewith, whatsoever hath betided. Yet would I say a word or two unto the woman that sitteth yonder. For I have been straying amongst wiles and images, and mayhappen I shall yet find this to be but a dream of the night, or a beguilement of the day." Therewith he arose from the table, and walked slowly down the hall; but it was a near thing that he did not fall a-weeping before all those aliens, so full his heart was.

He came and stood before the Hostage, and their eyes were upon each other, and for a little while they had no words. Then Hallblithe began, wondering at his voice as he spake: "Art thou a woman and my speech-friend? For many images have mocked me, and I have been encompassed with lies, and led astray by behests that have not been fulfilled. And the world hath become strange to me, and empty of friends."

Then she said: "Art thou verily Hallblithe? For I also have been encompassed by lies, and beset by images of things unhelpful."

"Yea," said he, "I am Hallblithe of the Ravens, wearied with desire for my troth-plight maiden."

Then came the rosy colour into the fairness of her face, as the rising sun lighteth the garden of flowers in the June morning; and she said: "If thou art Hallblithe, tell me what befell to the finger-gold-ring that my mother gave me when we were both but little."

Then his face grew happy, and he smiled, and he said: "I put it for thee one autumntide in the snake's hole in the bank above the river, amidst the roots of the old thorn-tree, that the snake might brood it, and make the gold grow greater; but when winter was over and we came to look for it, lo! there was neither ring nor snake, nor thorn-tree: for the flood had washed it all away."

Thereat she smiled most sweetly, and whereas she had been looking on him hitherto with strained and anxious eyes, she now beheld him simply and friendly; and she said: "O Hallblithe, I am a woman indeed, and thy speech-friend. This is the flesh that desireth thee, and the life that is thine, and the heart which thou rejoicest. But now tell me, who are these huge images around us, amongst whom I have sat thus, once in every moon this year past, and afterwards I was taken back to the women's bower? Are they men or mountain-giants? Will they slay us, or shut us up from the light and air? Or hast thou made peace with them? Wilt thou then dwell with me here, or shall we go back again to Cleveland by the Sea? And when, oh when, shall we depart?"

He smiled and said: "Quick come thy questions, beloved. These are the folks of the Ravagers and the Sea-eagles: they be men, though fierce and wild they be. Our foes they have been, and have sundered us; but now are they our friends, and have brought us together. And to-morrow, O friend, shall we depart across the waters to Cleveland by the Sea."

She leaned forward, and was about to speak softly to him, but suddenly started back, and said: "There is a big, red-haired man, as big as any here, behind thy shoulder. Is he also a friend? What would he with us?"

So Hallblithe turned about, and beheld the Puny Fox beside him, who took up the word and spoke, smiling as a man in great glee: "O maiden of the Rose, I am Hallblithe's thrall, and his scholar, to unlearn the craft of lying, whereby I have done amiss towards both him and thee. Whereof I will tell thee all the tale soon. But now I will say that it is true that we depart to-morrow for Cleveland by the Sea, thou and he, and I in company. Now I would ask thee, Hallblithe, if thou wouldst have me bestow this gift of thine in safe-keeping to-night, since there is an end of her sitting in the hall like a graven image: and to-morrow the way will be long and wearisome, What sayest thou?"

Said the Hostage: "Shall I trust this man and go with him?"

"Yea, thou shalt trust him," said Hallblithe, "for he is trusty. And even were he not, it is meet for us of the Raven and the Rose to do as our worth biddeth us, and not to fear this folk. And it behoveth us to do after their customs since we are in their house."

"That is sooth," she said; "big man, lead me out of the hall to my place. Farewell, Hallblithe, for a little while, and then shall there be no more sundering for us."

Therewith she departed with the Puny Fox, and Hallblithe went back to the high-seat and sat down by the Erne, who laughed on him and said: "Thou hast taken my gift, and that is well: yet shall I tell thee that I would not have given it to thee if I could have kept it for myself in such plight as thou wilt have it. But all I could do, and the Puny Fox to help withal, availed me nought. So good luck go with thine hands. Now will we to bed, and to-morrow I will lead thee out on thy way; for to say sooth, there be some here who are not well pleased with either thee or me; and thou knowest that words are wasted on wilful men, but that deeds may avail somewhat."

Therewith he cried out for the cup of good-night, and when it was drunken, Hallblithe was shown to a fair shut-bed; even that wherein he had lain aforetime; and there he went to sleep in joy, and in good liking with all men.

# CHAPTER XXII: THEY GO FROM THE ISLE OF RANSOM AND COME TO CLEVELAND BY THE SEA

In the morning early Hallblithe arose from his bed, and when he came into the mid-hall, there was the Puny Fox and the Hostage with him; Hallblithe kissed her and embraced her, and she him; yet not like lovers long sundered, but as a man and maid betrothed are wont to do, for there were folk coming and going about the hall. Then spake the Puny Fox: "The Erne is abiding us out in the meadow yonder; for now nought will serve him but he must needs go under the earth-collar with us. How sayest thou, is he enough thy friend?"

Said Hallblithe, smiling on the Hostage: "What hast thou to say to it, beloved?"

"Nought at all," she said, "if thou art friend to any of these men. I may deem that I have somewhat against the chieftain, whereof belike this big man may tell thee hereafter; but even so much meseemeth I have against this man himself, who is now become thy friend and scholar; for he also strove for my beguilement, and that not for himself, but for another."

"True it is," said the Fox, "that I did it for another; even as yesterday I took thy mate Hallblithe out of the trap whereinto he had strayed, and compassed his deliverance by means of the unfaithful battle; and even as I would have stolen thee for him, O Rose-maiden, if need had been; yea, even if I must have smitten into ruin the roof-tree of the Ravagers. And how could I tell that the Erne would give thee up unstolen? Yea, thou sayeth sooth, O noble and spotless maiden; all my deeds, both good and ill, have I done for others; and so I deem it shall be while my life lasteth."

Then Hallblithe laughed and said: "Art thou nettled, fellow-in-arms, at the word of a woman who knoweth thee not? She shall yet be thy friend, O Fox. But tell me, beloved, I deemed that thou hadst not seen Fox before; how then can he have helped the Erne against thee?"

"Yet she sayeth sooth," said Fox, "this was of my sleight: for when I had to come before her, I changed my skin, as I well know how; there are others in this land who can do so much as that. But what sayest thou concerning the brotherhood with the Erne?"

"Let it be so," said Hallblithe, "he is manly and true, though masterful, and is meet for this land of his. I shall not fall out with him; for seldom meseemeth shall I see the Isle of Ransom."

"And I never again," said the Puny Fox.

"Dost thou loathe it, then," said the Hostage, "because of the evil thou hast done therein?"

"Nay," said he, "what is the evil, when henceforth I shall do but good? Nay, I love the land. Belike thou deemest it but dreary with its black rocks and black sand, and treeless wind-swept dales; but I know it in summer and winter, and sun and shade, in storm and calm. And I know where the fathers dwelt and the sons of their sons' sons have long lain in the earth. I have sailed its windiest firths, and climbed its steepest crags; and ye may well wot that it hath a friendly face to me; and the land-wights of the mountains will be sorry for my departure."

So he spake, and Hallblithe would have answered him, but by now were they come to a grassy hollow amidst the dale, where the Erne had already made the earth-yoke ready. To wit, he had loosened a strip of turf all save the two ends, and had propped it up with two ancient dwarf-wrought spears, so that amidmost there was a lintel to go under.

So when he saw those others coming, he gave them the sele of the day, and said to Hallblithe: "What is it to be? shall I be less than thy brother-in-arms henceforward?"

Said Hallblithe: "Not a whit less. It is good to have brothers in other lands than one."

So they made no delay, but clad in all their war-gear, they went under the earth-yoke one after the other; thereafter they stood together, and each let blood in his arm, so that the blood of all three mingled together fell down on the grass of the ancient earth; and they swore friendship and brotherhood each to each.

But when all was done the Erne spake: "Brother Hallblithe, as I lay awake in bed this morning I deemed that I would take ship with thee to Cleveland by the Sea, that I might dwell there a while. But when I came out of the hall, and saw the dale lying green betwixt hill-side and hill-side, and the glittering river running down amidmost, and the sheep and kine and horses feeding up and down on either side the water: and I looked up at the fells and saw how deep blue they stood up against the snowy peaks, and I thought of all our deeds on the deep sea, and the merry nights, in yonder abode of men: then I thought that I would not leave the kindred, were it but for a while, unless war and lifting called me. So now I will ride with thee to the ship, and then farewell to thee."

"It is good," said Hallblithe, "though not as good as it might be. Glad had we been with thee in the hall of the Ravens."

As he spoke drew anigh the carles leading the horses, and with them came six of those damsels whom the Erne had given to Hallblithe the night before; two of whom asked to be brought to their kindred over sea; but the other four were fain to go with Hallblithe and the Hostage, and become their sisters at Cleveland by the Sea.

So then they got to horse and rode down the dale toward the haven, and the carles rode with them, so that of weaponed men they were a score in company. But when they were half-way to the haven they saw where hard by three knolls on the way-side were men standing with their weapons and war-gear glittering in the sun. So the Erne laughed and said: "Shall we have a word with War-brand then?"

But they rode steadily on their way, and when they came up to the knolls they saw that it was War-brand indeed with a score of men at his back; but they stirred not when they saw Erne's company that it was great. Then Erne laughed aloud and cried out in a big voice, "What, lads! ye ride early this morning; are there foemen abroad in the Isle?"

They shrank back before him, but a carle of those who was hindermost cried out: "Art thou coming back to us, Erne, or have thy new friends bought thee to lead them in battle?"

"Fear it nought," quoth Erne, "I shall be back before the shepherd's noon."

So they went their ways and came to the haven, and there lay the Flaming Sword, and beside her a trim bark, not right great, all ready for sea: and Hallblithe's skiff was made fast to her for an after-boat.

Then the Hostage and Hallblithe and the six damsels went aboard her, and when the Erne had bidden them farewell, they cast off the hawsers and thrust her out through the haven-mouth; but ere they had got midmost of the haven, they saw the Erne, that he had turned about, and was riding up the dale with his house-carles, and each man's weapon was shining in his hand: and they wondered if he were riding to battle with War-brand; and Fox said: "Meseemeth our brother-in-arms hath in his mind to give those waylayers an evil minute, and verily he is the man to do the same."

So they gat them out of the haven, and the ebb-tide drave out seaward strongly, and the wind was fair for Cleveland by the Sea; and they ran speedily past the black cliffs of the Isle of Ransom, and soon were they hull down behind them. But on the afternoon of the next day they hove up the land of the kindreds, and by sunset they beached their ship on the sand by the Rollers of the Raven, and went ashore without more ado. And the strand was empty of all men, even as on the day when Hallblithe first met the Puny Fox. So then in the cool of the evening they went up toward the House of the Raven. Those damsels went together hand in hand two by two, and Hallblithe held the Hostage by the hand; but the Puny Fox went along beside them, gleeful and of many words; telling them tales of his wiles and his craft, and his skin-changing.

"But now," quoth he, "I have left all that behind me in the Isle of Ransom, and have but one shape, and I would for your behoof that it were a goodlier one: and but one wisdom have I, even that which dwelleth in mine own head-bone. Yet it may be that this may avail you one time or other. But lo you! though I am thy thrall, have I not the look of a thrall-huckster from over sea leading up my wares to the cheaping-stead?" They laughed at his words and were merry, and much love there was amongst them as they went up to the House of the Raven.

But when they came thither they went into the garth, and there was no man therein, for it was now dusk, and the windows of the long hall were yellow with candle-light. Then said Fox: "Abide ye here a little; for I would go into the hall alone and see the conditions of thy people, O Hallblithe."

"Go thou, then," said Hallblithe, "but be not rash. I counsel thee; for our folk are not over-patient when they deem they have a foe before them."

The Puny Fox laughed, and said: "So it is then the world over, that happy men are wilful and masterful."

Then he drew his sword and smote on the door with the pommel, and the door opened to him and in he went: and he found that fair hall full of folk and bright with candles; and he stood amidst the floor; all men looked on him, and many knew him at once to be a man of the Ravagers, and silence fell upon the hall, but no man stirred hand against him. Then he said: "Will ye hearken to the word of an evil man, a robber of the folks?"

Spake the chieftain from the dais: "Words will not hurt us, sea-warrior; and thou art but one among many; wherefore thy might this eve is but as the might of a new-born baby. Speak, and afterwards eat and drink, and depart safe from amongst us!"

Spake the Puny Fox: "What is gone with Hallblithe, a fair young man of your kindred, and with the Hostage of the Rose, his troth-plight maiden?"

Then was the hush yet greater in the hall, so that you might have heard a pin drop; and the chieftain said: "It is a grief of ours that they are gone, and that none hath brought us back their dead bodies that we might lay them in the Acre of the Fathers."

Then leapt up a man from the end-long table nigh to Fox, and cried out: "Yea, folk! they are gone, and we deem that runagates of thy kindred, O new-come man, have stolen them from us; wherefor they shall one day pay us."

Then laughed the Puny Fox and said: "Some would say that stealing Hallblithe was like stealing a lion, and that he might take care of himself; though he was not as big as I am."

Said the last speaker: "Did thy kin or didst thou steal him, O evil man?"

"Yea, I stole him," quoth Fox, "but by sleight, and not by might."

Then uprose great uproar in the hall, but the chieftain on the high-seat cried out: "Peace, peace!" and the noise abated, and the chieftain said: "Dost thou mean that thou comest hither to give us thine head for making away with Hallblithe and the Hostage?"

"I mean to ask rather," said the Fox, "what thou wilt give me for the bodies of these twain?"

Said the chieftain: "A boat-load of gold were not too much if thou shouldst live a little longer."

Quoth the Puny Fox: "Well, in anywise I will go and bring in the bodies aforesaid, and leave my reward to the goodwill of the Ravens."

Therewith he turned about to go, but lo! there already in the door stood Hallblithe holding the Hostage by the hand; and many in the hall saw them, for the door was wide. Then they came in and stood by the side of the Puny Fox, and all men in the hall arose and shouted for joy. But when the tumult was a little abated, the Puny Fox cried out: "O chieftain, and all ye folk! if a boat-load of gold were not too much reward for the bringing back the dead bodies of your friends, what reward shall he have who hath brought back their bodies and the souls therein?"

Said the chieftain: "The man shall choose his own reward." And the men in the hall shouted their yeasay.

Then said the Puny Fox: "Well, then, this I choose, that ye make me one of your kindred before the fathers of old time."

They all cried out that he had chosen wisely and manfully; but Hallblithe said: "I bid you do for him no less than this; and ye shall wot that he is already my sworn brother-in-arms."

Now the chieftain cried out: "O Wanderers from over the sea, come up hither and sit with us and be merry at last!"

So they went up to the dais, Hallblithe and the Hostage, and the Puny Fox and the six maidens withal. And since the night was yet young, the supper of the men of the Ravens was turned into the wedding-feast of Hallblithe and the Hostage, and that very night she became a wife of the Ravens, that she might bear to the House the best of men and the fairest of women.

But on the morrow they brought the Puny Fox to the mote-stead of the kindreds that he might stand before the fathers and be made a son of the kindred; and this they did because of the word of Hallblithe, and because they believed in the tale which he told them of the Glittering Plain and the Acre of the Undying. The four maidens also were made sisters of the House; and the other twain were sent home to their own kindred in all honour.

Of the Puny Fox it is said that he soon lost and forgot all the lore which he had learned of the ancient men, living and dead; and became as other men and was no wizard. Yet he was exceeding valiant and doughty; and he ceased not to go with Hallblithe wheresoever he went; and many deeds they did together, whereof the memory of men hath failed: but neither they nor any man of the Ravens came any more to the Glittering Plain, or heard any tidings of the folk that dwell there.

Herewith endeth the Tale.

6727138R00061

Printed in Great Britain
by Amazon.co.uk, Ltd.,
Marston Gate.